Redemptio

Redemptions

A Costa Rican Novel

by Carlos Gagini

Translated by
E. Bradford Burns

with line drawings by
Francisco Amighetti

San Diego State University Press

Published by San Diego State University Press
San Diego, California 92182

English translation copyright © 1985
by San Diego State University Press
All rights reserved

Originally published in Spanish as *El Arbol Enfermo*,
Costa Rica, 1918.

Library of Congrsess Cataloging in Publication Data

Gagini, Carlos, 1865-1925.
Redemptions: A Costa Rican Novel.
Translation of: El árbol enfermo.
I. Title.
PQ7489.G27A913   1985   863   84-51946

ISBN 0-916304-66-3
ISBN 0-916304-67-1 (pbk.)

Cover illustration from a drawing by Francisco Amighetti
Book and cover design by Rachael Bernier

Contents

Translator's Introduction

Literature provides a window to a people's mind. Latin America's rich literature frames social, economic, and political preoccupations. The Latin Americans, in particular, have used their literature as one means to discuss the serious topic of national identity. Who are they? What are their roots, their destinies? Not surprisingly, many answers respond to these simple, yet vital and complex, questions.

Questions of national identity divided the Latin Americans after they achieved independence. Emphasizing ties with the Old World, one group advocated the recreation of Europe in Latin America. Others, arguing that Europe had contributed to only a part of the Latin American experience, cherished the characteristics that made Latin America unique. The debates between these groups constitute stimulating chapters in Latin American intellectual, cultural, and political history, and their varying points of view provide one of the most useful insights into an understanding of the Latin Americans.

Early generations of Latin American intellectuals inclined more toward European values. They averted their eyes from the local scene and the Iberian peninsula to gaze longingly toward London and—in particular—toward Paris. No one set the tone for the nineteenth century more forcefully than the Argentine Domingo F. Sarmiento. In his *Civilización y barbarie: vida de Juan Facundo Quiroga (Life in the Argentine Republic in the Days of the Tyrants: or Civilization and Barbarism; 1845)*, Sarmiento put forth the dialectic characteristic of so much of the nineteenth and even twentieth-century Latin American thought: the progress of the city with its Europeanized core contrasted with the ignorance and primitivism of the countryside, as yet unredeemed by Europe. The Old World represented civilization; the New World and anything native to it manifested barbarism. The best hope for the new American nations was a sound European education for their inhabitants and the encouragement of as many Europeans as possible to migrate to the Western Hemisphere. Subscribing to that fundamental notion obviously required the intellectuals to draw from Europe. That notion dominated nineteenth-century Latin American literature.

Only later in the century did questioning intellectuals effectively challenge the European preference. Readers cannot help but be struck by the powerful struggle in the minds of sensitive literati between the European theories they knew so well and the American realities they were only beginning to learn to appreciate. The masterpiece of Brazil's Euclides da Cunha, *Os Sertões (Rebellion in the Backlands,* 1902) illustrated that struggle. Da Cunha found himself in an agonizing dilemma over his admiration for the strength, courage, and skills of the impoverished people of the Brazilian interior and his European indoctrination emphasizing their inferiority. Da Cunha wavered. His nationalism aroused sympathy for the backlanders; his education ruled they must be Europeanized or eradicated. "We are condemned to civilization," he sighed. Still, the seeds of doubt had been planted. The intellectuals began to question whether Europe indeed possessed the only viable civilization.

Other thinkers were less certain that unique Latin American values had to give way to European and North American ways of life. In his *Ariel* (1900), the Uruguayan José Enrique Rodó dramatically contrasted the Latin Americans' spirituality and idealism with the materialism of the North Atlantic nations, particularly of the United States. He struck a chord of sympathy—and nationalism—that reverberated throughout the hemisphere. Young intellectuals rallied to his call to defend a spiritually superior culture. His vision of Latin America was simple: "Ariel triumphant signifies idealism and order in life, noble inspiration in thought, unselfishness in conduct, high taste in art, heroism in action, delicacy and refinement in manners and usages." That observation enjoyed immense popularity. It confirmed nationalist pride just as it strengthened nationalist thought. Rodó succeeded in stating a cultural ideal that challenged the acceptance of the cultural monopoly—and imperialism—of western Europe north of the Pyrenees and of the United States.

José Vasconcelos carried the new cultural manifestation one step farther. In his *La Raza Cósmica* (1925), that Mexican intellectual proclaimed the emergence of a new and superior race in Latin America, the "Cosmic Race." Defying European racial doctrine that preached the creation of inferior beings through racial mixture, Vasconcelos proudly announced a new race, the fusion of all others. Racial mixture provided strength and richness, he affirmed. His muddled arguments often defy logic; his facts sometimes are wrong. Yet, Vasconcelos provides a refreshing Latin American thesis with an audacity that commands respect. He argued the superiority of Latin American culture over Anglo-American: ". . . they committed the sin of destroying those races, while we assimilated them, and this gives us new rights and hopes for a mission without precedent in History." That mission is the fusion of all peoples ethnically and spiritually to create the new superrace.

The questioning of European ideologies by intellects of the stature of da Cunha; the delineating of a unique Latin American spirituality by Rodó; and the bold proclamation of the superiority of the new American "race" by Vasconcelos carried Latin America a long way from the slavish adoration of European cultures found in Sarmiento. It helped to liberate the Latin American mind, encouraging a freedom to experiment and a regional confidence that nurtured some of the most imaginative and vigorous intellects of the twentieth century: Miguel Angel Asturias, Jorge Luis Borges, Jorge Amado, Carlos Fuentes, Octavio Paz, Gabriel García Marques, Alejo Carpentier, Gabriela Mistral, Pablo Neruda, José Carlos Mariátegui, and Julio Cortzar. One could easily mention others.

This brief outline of the development of intellectual attitudes does not argue that the path from an overreliance on Europe to an American originality was either rectilinear or easy. That path was strewn with the sharp rocks of debate, recrimination, self-doubt, and ingrained feelings of inferiority.

Each Latin American nation debated the same fundamental nationalist questions, although not necessarily at the same time. Within Costa Rica's small intellectual community, for example, a lively debate over the role of nationalism in literature first erupted in 1894. The publication of Ricardo Fernández Guardia's first collection of short stories sparked the exchange. Reviewers, noting the strong French influences pervading the stories, lamented that they revealed so little of Costa Rica. The criticism rankled the young author, who responded testily to demand the literary freedom to draw inspiration from any source. Then he sarcastically concluded that barbarous Costa Rica, a country of only about 20,000 square miles and a quarter of a million inhabitants, offered neither inspiration nor worthy material for literature.[1]

Ideas had changed sufficiently by the end of the nineteenth century, however, that the praise of Parisian values and the disparagement of local ones no longer overawed all Costa Rican intellectuals. They did not inhibit the young Carlos Gagini (1865-1925), a contemporary of Fernández Guardia but an advocate of a more national approach to literature. Among his earliest published writings appear two pleas in the San José press for greater attention to national values and themes in Costa Rican literature.[2] The young teacher urged writers to "interpret the national spirit." For too long Latin Americans had disdained "national subjects" in favor of the exotic, the foreign, and the distant. Subservient to European models, the literature of the New World had not served Latin America's own best interests. The time had come for writers to pay at least some attention to the Costa Rican scene. Such attention would help the Costa Ricans to understand themselves and it might also contribute to a clearer statement and stronger defense of their values. Gagini followed his own advice. In 1898, he produced a slim volume of short stories, *Charasca,* which drew on local scenes, customs, and themes. He never wavered in his faith in the role literature could play in defining and redeeming national culture. Within the broader framework of Latin American intellectual and cultural history, his small voice formed part of a larger chorus encouraging a novel but extremely important goal. Within the narrower confines of Central America, however, Gagini played a proportionately more significant role, giving expression to the new nationalism of the emerging urban middle class, a group that would shape the twentieth-century history of that region.

Gagini entered into those spirited discussions at a critical moment, particularly for Central America. In the wake of Spain's defeat in 1898, the United States expanded more aggressively into the Caribbean. The rising wave of United States military interventions engulfed Panama in 1903, 1908, and 1912; Honduras in 1905, 1910, 1912, and 1924; and Nicaragua during the years 1909-1925 and again from 1926 to 1933. After helping to overthrow the highly nationalistic President José Santos Zelaya in 1909, the United States directly controlled Nicaragua for the next twenty-four years. While Washington directed the national bank, railroads, custom houses and ports, the Nicaraguan economy disintegrated.[3] That disintergration and the accompanying occupation disquieted the Costa Ricans who shared a frontier with Nicaragua. North Americans roaming around that neighboring republic inevitably envoked memories of the unsavory William Walker and his filibuster army of the mid-nineteenth century.[4]

Under those circumstances, Gagini turned his attention to the most pressing question of his time: the expanding United States presence and influence in Latin America. The dynamic growth and expansion of the "Colossus of the North" aroused a confused mixture of fear, dislike, admiration, and imitation, contradictions Gagini and many other Latin American nationalists expressed but never quite resolved. Questions of racial and cultural inferiority or superiority arose to bedevil the Central American intellectuals. They felt compelled to address those difficult issues. That compulsion promoted nationalism in literature. It also nurtured the "anti-imperialist novel" throughout Latin America. The first of that genre, *El Problema,* came from the pen of a Guatemalan, Máximo Soto Hall, in 1899. Gagini wrote the second, the slim, symbolic novel *El Arbol Enfermo* (1918), translated here as *Redemptions.*

Gagini addressed the issues of nationalism, imperialism, and cultural identity in *Redemptions.* The novel falls chronologically between the statements of Rodó and Vasconcelos. The influence of Rodó is unmistakable. In his own small corner of Latin America, Gagini helped to popularize the theme of Latin American spiritual superiority. More importantly, perhaps, he helped the Costa Ricans and Central Americans to turn their eyes inward, shunning European and North American influences in an effort to enliven local perspectives.

Certainly one of the primary reasons citizens of the United States should read a writer like Carlos Gagini in the late twentieth century is to get a Central American perspective of the role of the United States in the isthmus. As that role has not changed throughout this century, the insights offered by Gagini in 1918 retain their validity almost three-quarters of a century later. We desperately need to broaden both our perception and sensitivity. Gagini will help us to do both.

While Gagini's message clearly speaks to his late twentieth-century readers, his style retains the flavor of the early years of the century. Romanticism and realism combine in his prose—and some might add in his philosophy as well. Indeed, one major commentator on the Central American novel labels the style of the Costa Rican as "romantic realism."[5] This intertwining of two contradictory literary styles bears witness to the very colonial mentality Gagini and his peers denounced. Latin America spawned few indigenous literary styles. Contrary to European experience in which literary styles evolved more or less naturally, the Latin American writers simply imported their styles from abroad, often not even bothering to modify them to better suit local conditions. Neither assimilated nor superseded, the various and often contradictory literary styles existed side by side, and the Latin Americans simply drew on them with scant concern about their possible contradictions.

Romanticism died an agonizingly slow death in Latin America, given a longevity that lasted until well into the twentieth century by writers in the less cosmopolitan centers. Gagini drew on the passion, morality, and drama of romanticism. His novels instruct, enlighten, and judge. He used character types, felt comfortable with allegory, and embraced nature as an integral part of the action. Indeed, in *Redemptions,* the weather often set the mood. It framed the actions of protagonists with bright skies or cold drizzles.

Gagini emphasized the new social, economic, and political forces at work in Central America in general and in Costa Rica in particular. By the time Gagini published his novel, 1918, Costa Rica depended on the export of a single product, coffee, for its economic well being. Efforts to modernize the nation further contributed to its dependency. Foreigners took control of the national economy.

To market larger quantities of coffee and thereby earn the capital to modernize the nation, the governments during a twenty-year period (1870-1890) had encouraged the construction of a railroad linking the highlands, where the coffee grew, to Puerto Limón, from where the beans were shipped abroad. The loans contracted for the railroad overburdened the treasury as the government paid outrageous interest rates to unscrupulous foreign lenders. Further, the government bestowed on Chief Engineer Minor Keith 800,000 acres, land which fronted on the railroad and later became the center of the plantations of the United Fruit Company. Even so, the railroad remained in foreign hands. British investors also controlled the ports, mines, electric lighting, major public works, and foreign commerce as well as the principal domestic marketplaces. Costa Rica clearly had surrendered its economic independence and mortgaged its future, realities that greatly disturbed nationalists like Gagini and provided a bitter backdrop for *Redemptions*.

Present in the novel is also a significant new social reality: the emergence of very small urban working and middle classes during the opening decades of the twentieth century. Always remote from the activities of the Spanish empire and even isolated from the political turmoil of the rest of Central America, Costa Rica contained little wealth and engaged in minimal foreign trade until the last quarter of the nineteenth century. Consequently, no privileged wealthy class to speak of had existed. Poverty created a kind of equality in a nation which contained only slightly more than a quarter of a million inhabitants at the close of the century. The nation's disastrous experience with financing a railroad further constrained the acquisition of wealth. Costa Rica probably had a higher percentage of small and middle-range farmers than any other Latin American country at the end of the century. A society without the sharp edges of economic extremes offered good conditions for the growth of a middle class. The period from 1889 to 1917 boasted a remarkable record of constitutional government in which four-year presidential terms were honored and peacefully exchanged. Politicians and parties supported platforms substantively middle class in their goals. In the last half of the 1880's, Minister of Education Mauro Fernández laid the foundation for a system of free and compulsory public education that eventually would produce Latin America's most literate population. Likewise, the government began to pay greater attention to public health. The wide-spread medical and health care the government provided its citizens made them the healthiest of Central America. The relatively equitable pattern of land ownership, the positive emphasis on education, and the comparatively wide-spread participation of the citizenry in politics marked Costa Rica in the early twentieth century as a nation of middle class proclivities, contrasting it dramatically with the other Central American nations.

The political and economic stresses of a nation in the flux of modernization characterized the period in which Gagini wrote his novel. Minister of War General Federico A. Tinoco overthrew the constitutional government in January, 1917, charging it with corruption. Refusal of the government of President Woodrow Wilson to recognize Tinoco helped to dislodge him from power in August, 1919, after which Costa Rica returned to the formalities of constitutional government. Tinoco, however, represented less the military in power (exceedingly rare in Costa Rica after 1889) and more the instability of an economy disoriented by World War I and of politics increasingly pervaded by urban elements that sought to diminish the landowners' influence.

Gagini discussed the national problems of his time. He sought solutions for them. His characters spent much of their time analyzing such problems and suggesting solutions. Their dialogue not only expressed the ideas of the author but reflected the opinions of many of Latin

America's literati. The ideas fit well within the intellectual trends of the times. On this level, the novel remains a significant fictional documentary, offering an insight into Latin American opinion at a critical moment.

Gagini generously used symbolism in his discussions of national reality. Indeed, above all else, *Redemptions* is a symbolic novel. Dual symbols represent Costa Rica. One is the huge fig tree near the house on the estate of Rafael Montalvo. Taking immense pride in the great tree, Don Rafael loves to spend part of the day seated in its shade. Margarita, his daughter, also symbolizes the nation. Beautiful and charming, she is somewhat helpless, a victim of forces far stronger than she is. Interrelating both symbols as the human and natural symbols of Costa Rica, the author emphasizes to his reader that they represent two aspects of the same thing. Don Rafael planted the fig tree the day Margarita was born. He considered the two as twins. They suffered the same fate, the fate of Costa Rica, at least in the mind of Gagini. The tree, slowly rotting, needed corrective treatment; the woman, corrupted by a foreigner, needed redemption.

Thomas Ward, handsome, clever, energetic, is the foreign presence. A United States citizen who owns and manages businesses in Costa Rica, he introduces modernization, that is, outside attitudes and ways. Those innovations may bring some benefits, but they also corrupt. Perhaps like the U.S. railroad engineer Minor Keith, he promises progress but in reality creates more problems than he solves. Although Gagini fully appreciates the dilemmas brought into play, he never really resolves them. The foreigner attracts Margarita. She weakens, and he seduces her. She provides gratification to the foreigner but at the same time he rejects her. The foreigner has but one use for Costa Rica: exploitation.

The Costa Rican counterpart to the materialist Thomas Ward is the young, handsome, and intelligent Fernando Rodríguez, a political activist, writer, and lawyer.

He symbolizes both the national spirit and the hope for the future of Costa Rica. He is the instrumentality by which the nation will be redeemed. He loves Margarita. Her submission to Ward devastates him. In turn, the foreigner made Margarita miserable, lonely, isolated. She repeats to Fernando, "I'm alone . . . . I'm alone." Whatever his misgivings about her behavior, Fernando assumes part of the responsibility. The savior, Fernando rescues and redeems her.

The real redemption of Costa Rica requires the confrontation of Fernando Rodríguez and Thomas Ward. Their intricate interplay—between nationalism and foreign domination—gives the novel much of its substance and accounts for most of the interest it holds. From the beginning, the reader recognizes the different values each young man cherishes. Fernando, an expert rider, arrives at the Montalvo estate on horseback in the first chapter. He is a man of nature, linked at that moment to the customs of his country. Thomas drives a newly imported car to the estate. His familiarity with machinery connects him to the future. While Thomas makes business deals, Fernando devotes much of his time to writing a play exposing the corrupting influence of luxury on the elite. He states, "I deeply love my country, and for that reason I desire that it be the most moral, prosperous, and happy of nations. To realize that ideal, it is necessary to begin at once to correct the vices of our character." To carry out those goals, he becomes involved in organizing and directing a political party that draws heavily on the "people." It contrasts with the self-serving parties directed by the political hacks.

Fernando represents in his actions a complex series of forces and groups, some of which emerged only in the late nineteenth-century Latin America. He is an intellectual in a region of the world in which intellectuals have played major political roles, including occupying the presidency. He lives in the city and identifies with it. He understands the growing influence of San José, even though in 1917 it was a capital of only 40,000 inhabitants, about one-tenth of the nation's population. Still, Costa Rica, like Latin America, was urbanizing rapidly. Changing demography conferred ever greater power on the cities. In the cities, the middle class and an incipient proletariat were allying to exercise political power. Fernando is a lawyer. His profession and his urban residence define his political mission and alliances. Despite his wealth, his ideas associate him with the rise of the middle sectors in Costa Rican society. Fernando's political party with its "progressive" goals and broad electorate represents those sectors, a new political force. Gagini leads us to believe, through his use of Fernando, that a progressive urban middle class, supported by a subordinate working class, will redeem Costa Rica, a hope not unusual among intellectuals of the period. Unlike Don Rafael and Mr. Ward, both large landowners, Fernando professes no rural roots. The answers to Costa Rican problems do not lie in a return to the rural past. Yet, Fernando is not a repudiation of the past. He could not be if redemption was to be national. The future will be built parallel to but somehow not compromised by the patterns of the rural past. The young lawyer embodies a kind of nebulous compromise of past and present with the future, exactly as the middle sectors did and the middle class still does. Thus, Gagini subscribed to a kind of theory of historical evolution, and he perceived Costa Rica at an historic juncture at which new forces took control.

Both Rafael and Virginia Montalvo seem to represent the old and noble virtues of Costa Rica. They hover in the novel as the presence of the past. Both bear some responsibility for the disgrace of Margarita and thus of Costa Rica. Clearly, they, the past, do not have the means to redeem Margarita or to regenerate the nation. The Montalvos finally have to depend on Fernando and the forces he represents.

If Don Rafael symbolizes some virtues, he incarnates some vices as well. The rural patriarch allowed the old fig tree to rot, the implication being that the landed class had let Costa Rica degenerate or simply had not kept abreast of the changing times. The diseased tree finally falls, killing Don Rafael. He must bear the responsibility for his own death. The reader again confronts the Costa Rica symbol and redemption. In this second instance, the new Costa Rica will be nurtured—as we shall see—by the invigorated middle class in alliance with the equally small but likewise disproportionately vocal urban working class. Significantly, while the first half of the novel takes place largely in the countryside, the last half shifts to the city. That change foretells Gagini's plan for the solution of national problems.

As part of the process of redemption, Fernando wants to deflect the direct influence of the United States. He recognizes great qualities in the industrializing and expanding giant to the North. Still, he rejects the values, the way of life of that menacing power. Much of the novel focuses literally and symbolically on the different life styles characterizing Latin America and the United States. In that respect, the intricate interplay between Ward and Rodríguez gives the novel much of its substance and accounts for most of the interest it holds. Don Rafael also frets about U.S. influence despite his own fascination with its technology. He and Ward converse at length on the U.S. role in Latin America. Washington's military intervention in Nicaragua obviously offends the old gentleman. In Chapter X, Gagini cleverly combines talk with action, theory with practice. Montalvo and Ward discuss the implications of U.S. intervention in Central America. Ward details the weaknesses of Latin America, not neglecting to point out how some Latin Americans seem to invite, even welcome, the interventions. They want to behave like North Americans. They seek the same life style. Imitation facilitates the intervention. Gagini here blames the Latin Americans as much as the North Americans. The last part of the chapter symbolically illustrates his point as Ward makes advances to Margarita, who seems willing to submit. Her passivity encourages the Yankee entrepreneur.

Not least among the symbolic references is the date on which the team of United States soccer players defeats the Costa Rican team: April 11. It is the national holiday. On that date in 1856, Central Americans, among whom the Costa Ricans figured significantly, defeated an army of William Walker, the U.S. filibuster who terrorized and humiliated Central America in the mid-1850s. In the long and bloody battle of Rivas, Nicaragua on April 11, 1856, the Costa Ricans helped to check the advance of the filibusters. Ironically, Gagini chose that date for the soccer match and the triumph of the U.S. team captained by Thomas Ward.

Much of the novel directly or indirectly centers on the differences between Anglo and Latin cultures, an old discussion in Latin America greatly enlivened by the easy U.S. victory over Spain in 1898 and the physical expansion of the United States into the Caribbean. Buttressing the popular Rodó thesis, Gagini dwells on the materialism of the United States and the spiritual qualities of Latin America. Fernando comments during his exile in New York City that social visits seem to be extensions of business meetings, the conversations dwell on statistics and market prices. Still, ambiguities soften the degree of Gagini's cultural dichotomy. He obviously admires the freedom, order, efficiency, and technology of the United States, just as he laments the political bankruptcy, social vices, and educational malaise of Costa Rica. He makes a great point of stressing that Costa Rica's problems not be laid at the door of the United States, at least not in their entirety. Costa Ricans must take responsibility for their own future, one in which reform, nationalism, the city and the working and middle classes seem destined to play major roles. An understanding of Gagini's abundant use of symbolism helps the reader to appreciate the meaning of the novel.

In the final analysis, the importance of this novel lies in its frank discussion of problems and ideas that troubled Costa Ricans—and Latin Americans—during the early decades of the twentieth century. For that matter, these problems and ideas continue to attract attention; and, perhaps, they have never engendered as much concern as they do in the 1980s, when Central America stands on the threshold of major political, economic, and social changes and "Yankee" intervention again has become a reality. In his history of the Costa Rican novel, Rodrigo Solera concluded, "The contribution of Gagini to the Costa Rican novel was to give it an ideological dimension by writing the first 'thesis novels.' "[6]

Among the many reasons recommending the reading of *Redemptions*, literary merit does not figure. A kind of old-fashioned melodrama, the novel is unsophisticated literature. Gagini used the novel as the medium for a message. The message is far more important than the medium. *Redemptions* demonstrates that if we want to improve our understanding of Latin American thought we must diversify our sources. For too long we have concentrated on a couple of dozen outstanding Latin American writers and ignored the legions of others. To the extent we have done so, we have restricted our vision. In some respects, writers like Gagini better reflect Latin American concerns that do some of the talented literary giants. I suppose I risk protest if I suggest that for all his undeniable genius Jorge Luis Borges cannot be considered as a source of profound insight into Latin American reality. At any rate, we should balance the Borgeses with the Gaginis if we expect to achieve a more accurate understanding of Latin America.

Despite its obvious literary faults, *Redemptions* unexpectedly operates on a variety of levels of meaning. The first is as a story. The rather simple plot manages to hold the reader's interest largely because of the psychological development of the characters. Further, it offers a fascinating insight into both urban and rural life in Costa Rica during the second decade of the twentieth century.

Symbolism, however, gives the novel its fullest meaning. It is a valuable document detailing the Latin Americans' intensive search for self-definition and signifying the triumph of nationalism.

The novel is also a personal document, a partial autobiographical statement since Fernando embodies so many of the ideas of Carlos Gagini and even some of his experiences.[7] Gagini, an ardent nationalist, spent some years in self-exile. He visited both Spain and the United States, the two destinations of Fernando, and those nations represent a part of Costa Rica's past and future. He was suspicious of, even hostile toward, the United States: ". . . two weeks in the United States were sufficient to understand the differences between the Latin and Anglo-Saxon civilization, ours so eminently sensitive, generous, and unselfish, theirs so profoundly selfish, provincial and practical."[8]

The author, like his character Fernando Rodríguez had written a drama of instruction "to arouse the interest of our youth in the history of their country."[9] The National Theatre presented his work, and like Fernando's it enjoyed much success: "The enthusiasm of the public was indescribable. Seats sold for double and even triple their price and still the theatre was packed."[10]

Gagini took a dim view of politics, which he described as the art by which the few manipulate the many. He had exalted ideas of what Costa Rica should be: "I dream that my country will one day have a democratic government blessed with liberty and directed not by the whim of a single man but by the will of public opinion. Sad experience has taught me that we do not yet have the civic preparation for such a government. In the meantime, as we educate ourselves, what we need is a benevolent, progressive, honest, and energetic dictatorship that will guide our nation with a firm hand until that day when our people can govern themselves."[11] He lavishly praised the hardworking "artisan" class, a class, by the way, to which he was closely connected through his father, a carpenter.

Gagini himself always lived on the edge of poverty. A major step toward reform and growth was to point out national defects. "I always indicated defects, vices, and abuses so that they could be remedied," he confessed.[12] In fact he regarded this novel, *Redemptions,* as one of his major statements on Costa Rican political corruption: "I constantly called the attention of our young people to our political corruption as can be seen in my novel *El Arbol Enfermo.*" [13]

The long list of similarities between Gagini and his fictional character Fernando Rodríguez illustrates the very personal statement he was making in *Redemptions.* Decades of experience as a teacher, director of schools, and, on occasion, an employee of the Ministry of Education provided the background and insight for him to write this symbolic novel, a statement of criticism but also of hope for national redemption.

Notes

1   *El Heraldo de Costa Rica,* June 24, 1894. Margarita Castro Rawson reprints part of the debate in her *El costumbrismo en Costa Rica* (San José: Lehmann, 1981), pp. 321-335.

2   *Cuartillas,* May 28, 1894; *La República,* June 29, 1894.

3   Charles L. Stansifer, "José Santos Zelaya: A New Look at Nicaragua's 'Liberal' Dictator," *Revista/Review Interamericana* 7 (1977): 469, 479; Jaime Biderman, "The Development of Capitalism in Nicaragua: A Political Exonomic History," *Latin American Perspectives,* 10 (1983): 12.

4   Arriving in Nicaragua in June, 1855, Walker later declared himself president, contracted foreign loans using Nicaraguan lands as collateral, reinstituted slavery, and declared English the official language. The United States government recognized him as president.

5   Ramón Luis Acevedo, *La novela centroamericana. Desde el Popol-Vuh hasta los umbrales de la novela actual* (Río Piedras, Puerto Rico: Editorial Universitaria, 1982), p. 116. Acevedo also observed, "*El árbol enfermo* is one of the most representative novels of Central American realism from the beginning of this century. It is a novel of ideas. . . ." (p. 128).

6   Rodrigo Solera, "La Novela Costarricense" (Ph.D. dissertation, University of Kansas, 1964), p. 62.

7   Studies of Carlos Gagini are few. For a rather sketchy biography see Carlos Jinesta, *Carlos Gagini. Vida y obras* (San José: Lehman, 1936).

8   Carlos Gagini, *A través de mí vida* (San José: Editorial Costa Rica, 1976), p. 140.

9   Ibid., p. 138.

10 Ibid.

11 Ibid., p. 132.

12 Ibid., p. 133.

13 Ibid., p. 135.

Redemptions

La Cordillera
Amighetti -31-

I

The Estate

THE HORSE RACED ON, its elegant neck arched, its ears erect. its black coat shining with sweat. The polished bridle glistened through the rising dust. Beneath the spirited gallop, the surface of the road resounded. From the huts scattered along both sides of the road rushed a tattered band of kids, their faces rather more healthy than clean. Equal measures of curiosity and distrust propelled them. The women, occupied with morning duties but still attracted by the regular and vigorous rhythm of a fine horse, appeared discretely at their kitchen windows. They could not confuse the sound they heard with the usual lumbering noises of the country nags.

Absorbed in his thoughts, the rider remained oblivious to the stares. He sat erect in the saddle, his coat buttoned to his chin. A slight nod of his head acknowledged the greetings from an endless line of milkmen headed toward the city with their huge containers of milk.

The little road, always climbing, passed in a straight line through the town of Guadalupe, emerged from the coffee zone, divided in two the village of San Isidro, and then zigzagged through farms and meadows. Finally, hidden beneath the trees, it disappeared into the forests crowning the mountains.

Behind the rider a dazzling panorama slowly opened. To the north, the Barba Mountains and to the south the Aserri Mountains stretched out like the jaws of a pair of pliers whose axis was the Irazú Volcano. In the center of the expansive valley lay San José, the capital, like an urban island in a verdant agrarian sea. Along the mountainside small villages of whitewashed houses resembled piles of seashells thrown against the rocks. To the west where the enormous jaws of the pliers had not quite closed, the blue hills of the coast hid the Gulf of Nicoya. The eye could easily distinguish on the slopes and in the glens the varied uses of land: the yellow blotches of sugar plantations, the green squares of coffee estates, the wide meadows with their grazing herds, the silver threads of rivers, and the ruddy brush ready to be burned.

On a morning such as that one, the countryside bathed in the light of the rising sun could not be more attractive, but the rider must have been accustomed to that sight because his thoughts concentrated on the other matters. Not once did he turn his head to contemplate the beauty of the valley.

He was a young man of twenty-eight with a lightly tanned complexion, extremely dark eyes and hair, and an intense look which might have given him a certain hardness were it not for his sensitive mouth and rather tender expression. Of ordinary height, slim but strong, he revealed in both dress and manner that distinction readily visible in true gentlemen. His well-manicured hands and his muscular arms indicated that while he took good care of his body his primary concern was with the intellect.

The road became steeper and lonelier. Stones replaced the dust over which the horse had trotted. The noble animal showed no signs of fatigue, nor did it ever break step. Suddenly at the top of a hill, it turned to the left like one who knows the land well to follow a path shaded by two lines of orange trees whose branches hung heavily laden with the fruit.

Like someone who had suddenly awakened, the rider raised his eyes. The recognition of these surroundings filled him with joy. Sitting upright in the saddle, he wiped his face with his handkerchief and then brushed off his clothing. In a couple of minutes he stopped at an iron gate which he opened without dismounting.

About a hundred feet from there in the midst of a meadow stood an elegant and spacious adobe house of one story. A large garden surrounded it. A stately old fig tree dominated that beautiful landscape.

The western side of the house boasted an ample veranda with sliding stained glass windows, supported by iron columns painted white and crowned by golden capitals. A multitude of flower pots displaying a dazzling variety of plants adorned the veranda furnished with rattan chairs and sofas and little lacquer tables. Above the veranda a terrace with a jasper balastrade offered an admirable view of the magnificent panorama already described as well as in the opposite direction a view of the bleak cone of Irazú, blackened by eruptions.

Behind the house stood other more modest buildings: the stables, cowsheds, and the necessary barns of an estate. Farther on, the scene exposed hills and fields covered with a luxuriant green.

The rider dismounted at the foot of the marble stairs to the veranda. A worker hurried to take the reins and lead the horse to the stable.

"Tell Fermín not to wash Menelik until he cools down," the rider ordered. And then, catching sight of the closed door to the house, he asked, "Hasn't the family gotten up yet?"

"I don't think Miss Margarita has," responded the worker as he unbridled the horse," "but Doña Virginia is in the dining room. Shall I tell her you've arrived?"

"Don't say anything for the moment. I'm going to stroll in the garden. And where's Don Rafael?"

"He's riding around the estate with some foreigner."

"A foreigner?"

"Yes. Some gentleman arrived on foot a short while ago."

The worker led the horse away and the former rider, after wandering briefly along the garden paths, sat down on a bench, took a pencil and pad from his pocket and prepared to write. No lovelier place could be imagined than that well-cared-for garden with its beds of rose bushes of every imaginable variety, its borders of carnations, white lillies, and jasmines, with edgings of violets and geraniums, in the midst of which could be seen here and there white and red camelias, lillies, and nards of exquisite perfume. One heard no other noise that the distant bellowing of cattle, the splashing of the spouts of the rustic fountains, and the hum of bees who enjoyed the rich banquet provided by nature and aided by art.

The morning visitor wrote a few lines, put down the pencil, and mechanically moved his lips from time to time, glancing at the windows of the house. They remained closed. Suddenly he heard footsteps and a voice asking, "What are you doing here so early?"

He quickly turned his head to find two people. One, the speaker, was a man of about sixty, tall, lean, a large aquiline nose, and all those features that recalled an old Castillian noble. His hair and mustache were completely white, and he was dressed in a long grey topcoat with a cap of the same color. His companion was a very tall young man, robust with a ruddy complexion, clean shaven, blond with huge blue eyes, in short a magnificent example of the Anglo-Saxon race.

The surprised young man stood up and affectionately shook the hand of the old man, who turning to the foreigner at his side said, "Mr. Ward, I have the honor of introducing you to one of the best lawyers, Don Fernando

Rodríguez. . . . What's this?" he asked when he caught sight of the pad and pencil the young man held. "Are you writing? Composing some verses perhaps?"

"This man," he continued directing his words to the Anglo-Saxon, "is also one of the most distinguished writers of our country and he already has published several books."

Mr. Ward bowed slightly again and spoke with an ambiguous smile, "I've had the pleasure of reading some of your work in the newspapers as well as the merited praise which the critics have bestowed on them" He spoke in excellent Spanish with only the slighest English accent. His pronunciation indicated that he must have lived for a long time in Latin America.

The three sat down in the shade of the fig tree and the conversation touched on a number of subjects. After a few minutes, the foreigner got up to leave.

"What! Aren't you going to stay and have lunch with us?" the old man asked.

"It's not possible. I have some urgent business in the capital."

"All right, we'll excuse you this time," replied Don Rafael, "but you are invited for Sunday. I imagine," he continued directing these remarks to Fernando, "Mr. Ward had to leave his automobile along the way because he couldn't ford the river. Just a minute, and I'll order the stableboys to saddle a horse for you."

"Thanks, but please don't bother. I'm used to walking long distances and for me its a pleasure to exercise my legs. Besides, the auto isn't that far away."

While the owner of the estate accompanied the American to the gate, Fernando returned to strolling through the garden. He abruptly stopped to look toward the house. The door had just opened and two women descended the stairs moving toward the lawyer. The first one was an extremely beautiful young lady, rather taller than shorter, with chestnut hair, large brown eyes shaded by long lashes, a straight nose, and full lips. Her rapid though graceful walk betrayed an unusual nervousness and the movement of her lithe and shapely body was almost feline. She dressed simply in white with a red sash, her only adornment a bunch of violets and a rosebud fastened on her chest with a diamond pin. Following her came an older lady of about sixty, thin, intelligent looking, and much given to joking. Her features looked astonishingly similar to those of Don Rafael.

"Shame on you!" said the young one, shaking the hand of the recent arrival. "You didn't tell us you were here."

"I arrived so early that I didn't think you were awake."

"Mama saw you from the dining room window and told me you were out here."

"I didn't come out to greet you," the old woman said with a smile, "because you were writing with such enthusiasm that I didn't want to interrupt you. Were you working on your play?"

"No, just some silly thoughts I had as I enjoyed this poetic scene."

"And who were they about, if I may be so bold," teased Margarita.

The lawyer blushed like a schoolboy and was about to answer when Don Rafael returned.

"Did the foreigner already leave?" Doña Virginia asked him.

"Yes, unfortunately he had to walk. Didn't you meet him before?" he added, directing the question to Fernando.

"I know his name. Was this his first visit here?"

"No, he's been here three times this week. He wants me to sell my plantation La Ceiba in Nicoya. I don't know. What do you think? It's a splendid piece of property. It covers more than four thousand acres, has its own natural port, good water, a healthy climate, plenty of wood, and excellent farm land. Mr. Ward has organized a company that wants to plant cotton and henequen in order to build a textile factory later. He certainly has a convincing way of proposing a business deal. We, with our vagueness, confuse the issues while he presents them clearly and asks for direct answers. Those go-getters are real devils!"

"That makes them unpleasant," Margarita observed. "I just don't like mechanical men who speak only of numbers."

"But you don't mind young men who speak in verse," Doña Virginia mischievously interjected.

This time it was Margarita who turned beet red.

"Let's go have a cup of coffee," said Don Rafael. "Our stroll gave me an appetite. Anyway, it's chilly out here."

The two young people conversing in low tones slowly moved toward the house, accompanied by the older couple. The aroma of coffee and tortillas with beans and cheese greeted them at the door to the dining room. Don Rafael spoke: "Today's Saturday. Fernando, you must stay until tomorrow. There's nothing to do in the city on Sunday, and anyway I need you to help study Mr. Ward's proposal." The lawyer offered some excuses, more for the sake of formality than anything else. The look that he gave the beautiful Margarita displayed the pleasure he felt in remaining at the country estate for the weekend.

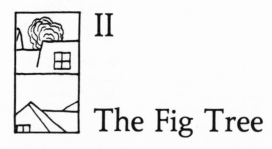

II

The Fig Tree

A<small>FTER LUNCH</small>, Don Rafael and his guest left the house to smoke cigars underneath the leafy fig tree in the garden. That giant tree towered above a circular patio of grass enclosed by a low hedge of cypress trees which, while it hid the two from the gaze of those in the house, still afforded a view of the marvellous panorama of the central plateau below. The whitened grey trunk, fluted like the pillars of Gothic cathedrals, boasted heavy parallel folds that rose straight to the point where the branches began and descended in twisting but artful curves until they were lost in the soil like some powerful tentacles of a monstrous antediluvian beast. The strong branches extended straight outward from the trunk like the arms of a fighter who had just delivered a blow. Lichen and parasites spotted those branches. The trunk supported a complex web of branches and a cupola of small, shiny, dark-green and reddish leaves through which the sun's rays struggled vainly to penetrate. In that labyrinth of geometric design created by the branches, birds hopped, fluttered, or battled with a deafening din.

With his own hand, Don Rafael had planted that tree the very day his only daughter Margarita had been born. Since then he cared for that tree with such love and attention that Doña Virginia had remarked, "My brother considers that fig tree to be the male twin of the girl, and he's almost annoyed with me because I don't treat it as I would a nephew."

Rare was the day when the owner of the estate didn't spend a couple of hours in the shade of that colossal tree and not infrequently lunch was served there. His affection for the tree was such that he forbade pruning or the slightest incision in the trunk. An excellent employee was fired because he dared once to hang up his machette by driving the blade into the trunk.

That magnificent example of Costa Rican flora was famous, not only in the immediate environs but even in the capital. It gave its name to the entire estate—El Higuerón— whose 450 acres of pastures grazed cattle of pure English, Swiss and North American breeds.

Don Rafael Montalvo, son of one of the most affluent farmers of the country, had taken courses during his youth in the old College of Cartago. Aware that studies did not suit his temperament, he abandoned them, much as Hernán Cortés had done. He left the classroom, however, not to conquer lands at sword's point but to cultivate them with the blade of the plow. Under his expert direction and immediate care, the estate acquired an immense value and its products enjoyed a well deserved fame in both national and international markets. At a mature age, he married a distinguished young lady from San José, who died three years later in childbirth. Doña Virginia, the twin sister of Don Rafael, took charge of the child's upbringing. Just because he lived in the country most of the year didn't mean that Don Rafael was not interested in what went on in the rest of the world. To the contrary, he received numerous visitors at the estate, especially on Sunday. He subscribed to a wide variety of European magazines. When the torrential rains began to fall in September, he went to the capital to spend several months in the beautiful home he maintained there. At that time he attended parties and frequented the theatre. His few moments of leisure were spent reading or listening to his daughter play the piano and sing.

His library, although not large, was well selected, boasting of the Spanish classics, in particular the mystics and playwrights, whom Don Rafael esteemed more than all the other writers of the world. He had no affection for the modern poets, whose verses he characterized as ridiculous, artificial, and immoral. Precisely because he found a certain analogy between the contemporary trends of modernism and the affectations of Calderón de la Barca, the author of *La Vida Es Sueño* did not enjoy his full approbation. On the other hand, he read and reread Cervantes, although because of his lack of philological training he didn't always understand the depths of that work, an inexhaustible mine of suggestive thoughts. He knew by heart entire scenes from the witty comedies of Ruiz de Alarcón, in whose characters, models of magnanimity and nobility, he doubtlessly found reflected his own sentiments.

Don Rafael Montalvo incarnated those splendid virtues of old Costa Rican gentlemen: little-educated, yet wise and prudent; religious without being a fanatic; generous without being lavish; honest in every respect, uncompromising with laziness, lies, vices, and dishonesty; faithful to his word; punctual in fulfilling his promises; a patriot without making a show of it; gallant without bragging; courteous but not obsequious; and respectful without fawning.

Doña Virginia, like all the women of her generation, received no more education than the fundamentals of primary school. She overcame those deficiencies with frequent reading, her keen insight, careful observation, astuteness of judgment, and above all with her good humor that neither the long years as a spinster nor advancing age had dimmed. Her deep religious convictions didn't prevent her from being tolerant with disbelievers nor from accompanying her niece—whom she always referred to as her little daughter—to dances and parties at which both young and old surrounded her, attracted by her lively conversation. All repeated her jokes and appreciated her insights. Indeed, her arrival often animated dull gatherings. At one of them a young dandy inquired of her, "What do you think of trousers for women, Doña Virginia?" She replied, "Well, in an age in which men wear corsets and are known to put on powder and rouge, I find nothing unusual about women wearing pants."

Margarita was admired for her beauty, natural grace, and unaffected flirtatiousness. If from her father she had inherited some of the noble qualities that characterized the Montalvos, from her mother she received an extremely nervous temperament that revealed itself in the vivacity of her movements and in fluctuating moods that disoriented all who knew her. She seemed somewhat impulsive, perhaps too fickle in her emotions. She could easily change from laughter to tears, changes that seemed without explanation. Yet, at other times, she remained passive before a pitiful scene. At school she had been well known for her pranks and her large number of boyfriends, students like herself, whom she infuriated with her inconstancy. Her fickleness began to diminish only some years later when she met Fernando Rodríguez at a dance. His gallant behavior, fine manners, and meaningful conversation captivated her and likewise impressed Doña Virginia who had systematically opposed all the other suitors of her niece.

Fernando, the only child of a rich widow, had finished his professional studies in Belgium. The same year of his graduation he received the unhappy news of his mother's death. More to please her than himself he had studied law, but his sensitive nature inclined him more toward the arts, especially literature. As his abundant income from rents permitted him to live comfortably, he spent more time in the company of the muses than of lawyers. The literati rather than clients frequented his offices.

Intelligent, judicious, and a sharp observer, he did not consider literature as a mere passtime but as a serious and noteworthy profession open only to the most intelligent. Literature, he believed, required the most serious preparation. Margarita was the first women to awaken his love. Reserved, master of himself and his sentiments, he didn't manifest his feelings with the usual signs of passion. Perhaps that circumspection bordering on coldness attracted the young woman and awoke in her feelings of love. One frequently observes the attraction of opposites as if the law of equilibrium that rules the physical world transcends also the moral.

The capricious moods of his beloved disturbed Fernando. He attributed them to the excessive love and liberty that surrounded her as she grew up. Exercising care, he made it a point to present himself in the house as a simple friend, an opportunity that gave him a chance to observe her at close hand before formally declaring his love.

Don Rafael appreciated the approach of the young suitor. He knew his background well and found in it no greater faults than Fernando's high idealism and his lack of interest in increasing his already abundant riches. The well-to-do farmer quickly came to admire the lawyer and entrusted to him all his judicial matters. As the young man visited the estate each week, the old man took advantage of the opportunity to chat for hours about his favorite authors. The time spent on them annoyed Margarita, whose jealousy actually caused her to detest them.

Although the two old folks had complete confidence in Fernando's intentions, the two young people rarely saw each other without the company of Don Rafael and much less without the inquisitional stares of Doña Virginia who might have modified many of her views to fit new times but never accepted the modern custom of leaving lovers alone. When her brother, more liberal than she, reprimanded her for her constant vigilance, Doña Virginia invariably responded, "Who removes temptation, removes danger."

Few afternoons equaled the beauty of that Saturday. The transparent air, very common in that climate, allowed one to distinguish the simple profile of the buildings of the distant city and the contours of the trees crowning the crests of the mountains stood out against the brilliant background of the sky like some distant black glyphs. The sun began to sink behind the coastal peaks and the enormous red glow seemed to float in a lake of molten lead. Seated on the granite bench that encircled the fig tree like an ashen ring, Don Rafael gazed at the majestic scene over the cypress hedge; Doña Virginia, seated nearby on a rustic bench, knitted; the two young people conversed quietly.

"How are the rehearsals of your play going?"

"They're pretty far advanced. Tomorrow they will announce the date of the opening which will be Saturday, a week from today. Will you attend?"

"Of course. We'll all go, even Fermín. But tell me, when you are backstage don't you talk with those actresses? They say there are two very pretty ones."

"Pretty or ugly, I only talk with them to make some observations about their interpretations of their roles."

"When I think about that I have a fit! Also, you have annoyed me because you refuse to discuss the plot of your play."

"Ah, if you knew it ahead of time, the play would seem even worse than it is when you see it."

Margarita was about to protest when her father approached, exclaiming, "These binoculars are wonderful. You couldn't have given me a better gift Fernando. I can see perfectly the train from Puerto Limón when it arrives in San José and also the streetcar of Guadalupe. Both of those worthwhile enterprises, like so many in this country, are in the hands of foreigners."

"Unfortunately you're right, but we're the ones to blame," said Fernando. "No one wants to risk any of his capital in any kind of entreprise, and yet we complain because foreigners get rich at our expense.

"That doesn't apply to me," responded Don Rafael somewhat annoyed. "As you know, on various occasions, I've proposed to my friends that we form companies for business, but no one seconds my idea."

"Yes, I well remember your efforts. If this country only had a dozen capitalists who think as you do, our nation would be far better off than it is."

"What envy I have of those daring entrepreneurs who fear nothing and try everything!" said Don Rafael. "Here you have this diabolical Mr. Ward, who before making me an offer on my lands in Nicoya, went to see them, walked across them in every direction, studied the roads and anchorage, and made a copy of the survey. Do you know what he said to me this morning? 'I've made all my calculations. Six months after we sign the sale, the rails will be laid and the machinery installed. Within a year we'll sell our first textiles.' What do you think of that?"

Fernando said nothing for a few minutes and then replied gravely, "I deeply love my country and for that reason I desire that it be the most moral, prosperous, and happy of nations. To realize that ideal it is necessary to begin at once to correct the vices in our character. Since I can't aspire to accomplish such an immense task, I content myself by denouncing the evils, using literature as an instrument to implant my ideas in the conscience of the people. As Faguet said, 'He is not a patriot who does not point his finger at the wounds from which his country suffers.' It is a thankless task, I know, but I must do it with resolution, like a sacred duty. My first play has as its theme one of our worst vices: the pursuit of luxury."

"And what title have you given it?" asked Don Rafael.

"At the Edge of the Precipice."

Night was falling. Everyone got up to return to the house. On the way, Don Rafael, who had remained a few steps behind the lawyer, spoke, "May I give you some advice? Don't become the redeemer. No one likes to have his defects thrown in his face and least of all the Costa Ricans. That's the way we are and that's the way we will always be."

III

The Premiere

FOR FERNANDO, the work preceding the premiere of his play kept him busier than he had ever been. Besides the two daily rehearsals, he had to resolve some of the difficulties the director, actors, and stage hands encountered with the stage machinery, scenery, and costumes. As a special favor, some reporters from the press were admitted to the final rehearsals after the author had urged them to be very discreet, knowing how much they could detract from the impact of the premiere by spreading their views of the play, and even giving away the plot. For the most part they followed his advice. Every day the newspapers carried some notices informing the public of the progress of the rehearsals, the luxury of the production, and even the number of tickets sold. They encouraged the expectations of the public and only added to the tension Fernando experienced. "What barbarians!" he exclaimed to some of his journalistic friends who had been praising his work. "You will convince the public that they are really going to see a great show and their disappointment is going to be all the more bitter."

Tempted at times to call off the premiere, he almost was sorry that he'd written the play when he saw how the actors mangled his poor lines or didn't interpret their roles the way he had imagined the characters of his drama should be. Fortunately, the producer, who was not unaware of the high esteem the author enjoyed and of the profits to be earned from the drama's success, was determined that the work succeed and exerted firm control over his subordinates. The final dress rehearsal was excellent. Doubtless contributing to the enthusiasm with which the actors worked was the knowledge that not only had every ticket been sold but that the scalpers received record-breaking prices for the few tickets they offered.

Finally Saturday night arrived. Fernando remained backstage from seven o'clock on in order to give final instructions and to oversee the last details. Trembling, he felt feverish, like a general at the solemn moment before leading the charge into battle. He moved from one side of the stage to the other, one moment answering endless questions from the actors and stage hands, the next studying the auditorium through the peep hole in the curtain to watch it slowly fill up. Through that hole, he recognized the faces of a thousand friends and acquaintances and saw in the boxes beautifully dressed matrons and young ladies. In one he spotted Margarita accompanied by her father, aunt, two friends, Luisa and Matilde Valdés, members of one of the finest families of the capital.

The young lady showed her own nervousness by folding and unfolding her fan and the rapid movement of her beautiful head, which turned each second as she chatted with one or another of her companions. She sat back from the rail of her box as if she feared the public and almost as if the constant gaze of opera glasses focused in her direction offended her.

From behind the curtain, the chatter of the crowd sounded to Fernando like the roar of an angry mob demanding his head. The clock struck eight. The bell gave its third and final call. The actors took their places. Slowly the curtain rose.

Fernando, hidden backstage, watched what took place on the stage as if it were a vision, a dream. He saw the shadowy children of his imagination take the form of human beings. They spoke, they gesticulated, they moved with thousands of eyes fixed on them and while thousands of minds united to the poet's by the magical thread of art shared the same emotions. Suddenly fear seized him and he nearly fled the theatre to take refuge in his house as though he were a criminal fleeing his crime. He had dared to discuss on the stage for that select audience to hear one of the most pervasive and disastrous social vices. Would that public patiently receive the hard lesson suggested in those scenes written by his fine pen? Would they empathize with the victims of that senseless passion that ruled the rich, corrupted the poor, and perverted the youth?

The plot developed naturally and logically. The audience continued to be attentive. The drama revealed to all the strong attraction of luxury as well as the tragedy it could bring. An innocent girl bedazzled by it allowed herself to be seduced. She had been an honest and happy wife, but her vanity awakened by the desire for luxury demanded from her impoverished husband clothing he could not afford in order to enhance her beauty.

Prolonged applause greeted the end of the first act, but to Fernando the reaction seemed cold and distant, too restrained. He didn't dare to appear during intermission. He sent a note to his beloved and peeked through the curtain to watch members of the audience discussing the first act in a lively fashion.

The first scenes of the second act went by in silence. The young author, thinking his work to be a hopeless failure, hurried to the stage door to escape, but at the very moment thunderous applause rocked the theatre. He heard people rushing toward him from the stage and before he knew what was happening he felt himself taken hold of and pulled by women's hands.

"Come on! Hurry up! The audience wants you on stage," the actresses shouted. And Fernando unexpectedly found himself before the large audience that cheered and applauded enthusiastically. The play was saved. After the last curtain call, friends of the playwright invaded the backstage area to congratulate him. Among them was Don Rafael.

"Bravo! Magnificent!" he exclaimed, giving the author a warm embrace. "My family sends you a thousand congratulations, although they wish you could have gone to greet them."

"When the play is over, I will accompany you to your house, but it didn't seem prudent to appear until I saw how it would be received."

"You're quite right. What a drama and what verses, my friend! They are worthy of Alarcón! My daughter cried two or three times and both Virginia and I got lumps in our throats." The old man continued to praise the work until the bell sounded for the third act. The audience was all caught up in the drama according to the delighted producer, and the poetic scenes of the third act were repeatedly interrupted by enthusiastic clapping. But the enthusiasm reached its height when finally the wife lured by luxury recovered her senses just in time to avert disaster. She returned to her husband's side and to a life of privations to which her vengeful seducer condemned her, but he received a just punishment for his outrageous behavior. Never has the theatre in Costa Rica heard a similar ovation. The author, brought forward by the principal actresses, was deliriously acclaimed while hats and bouquets rained down on the stage in spite of the theater rules. Fernando was carried in triumph to the foyer, and he had great difficulty in freeing himself from his admirers in order to get to the box of Don Rafael.

Palid, shaking, and without speaking a word, Margarita rose to greet Fernando. The silent reprimand of

her expression disappeared at once to be replaced by a more intense emotion, the supreme happiness of seeing her beloved converted into a public idol crowned by a halo of glory, of finding herself admired, envied, because the popular poet deposited at her feet all his laurels. She extended her hands lovingly. In the cloakroom of the box, while Fernando put her coat over her shoulders, she offered him her lips. The long and passionate kiss, their first, was the most important reward the artist received.

In the corridor they encountered Mr. Ward who had come to congratulate the poet, and they all left the theater together. As it was a splendid evening, Margarita suggested that they return on foot. Anyway, they couldn't all fit into the carriage and they had to accompany the Valdés sisters to their residence. But what Margarita really wanted was to spend some extra time with her sweetheart. Fernando extended his arm to her and under the cover of her fur coat he took hold of her gloved hand which he held throughout the walk home. Behind the couple, the American accompanied the two friends of Margarita, while Don Rafael and his sister brought up the rear.

The groups gathered on the street corners greeted the happy poet with congratulatory words, and the attractive couple overheard along the way snatches of conversation all about the same theme: the magnificent success of the drama. Margarita wouldn't have exchanged that night to be an empress. Never had she ever shown herself to be so expansive or so in love.

"Listen," she said, "on Tuesday they will repeat your play but if you go backstage I'll be furious. Don't you think I saw how those naughty actresses squeezed your hand when they pulled you on stage?"

Fernando laughed at her comments and promised never to set foot backstage again and even promised not to write another play in order to avoid giving her any cause for displeasure. He felt very happy. But his happiness was not for his dramatic triumph so much as for the passion which, for the first time, he observed in the eyes of his beloved and for that kiss whose sweet taste his mouth still savored. Beneath a reserved and cold exterior, Fernando sheltered a fine soul capable of the most extremes. When he fell in love with Margarita, he feared not to encounter in her a temperament of sufficient passion, but that night his doubts vanished and he was convinced that he could not have selected a more appropriate lover. How short the walk seemed even with the detour to leave the Valdes sisters at their door. On arriving at his home, Don Rafael said to Fernando, "Early tomorrow we return to the country because I want us to celebrate your triumph there with a family dinner. I hope you'll do us the honor of joining us," he added directing those final words to Mr. Ward.

Both men accepted the invitation, and the foreigner, on taking leave, offered Fernando a ride in his automobile.

"Many thanks," the lawyer answered with a smile, "but I can't accept your kind offer because I'm more certain of getting there on my horse Menelik."

The farewell of the two lovers was prolonged and would have been even longer if Doña Virginia hadn't ended it with one of her customary witticisms, "Children, this fourth act of the drama is turning out to be much longer than the others. The time has come to drop the curtain."

 IV

Conversations

By NINE IN THE MORNING the family was back at El Higuerón. Doña Virginia was about to begin preparations for the meal, while Margarita was seated, book in hand, in one of the chairs on the porch. Her attention wandered, her eyes traveled continuously between the pages of the book and the rows of orange tree that shaded the entrance to the estate. On a nearby table she had placed the binoculars. From time to time she used them to scrutinize the town of San Isidro, whose dusty street contrasted sharply with the green countryside. Shortly after ten a small, dark figure appeared on the horizon and moved rapidly in the direction of El Higuerón. Margarita's heart jumped, and even before she raised the glasses, her intuition told her who it was. She closed the book, retired briefly to her room to see how she looked, and then returned to lean against the rail of the porch.

Riding his spirited horse, Fernando arrived at the foot of the stairs where Don Rafael greeted him. He had seen the young man's arrival from his office, whose window looked out across the porch, garden, and entry to the estate. Margarita avoided the glance of her boyfriend, and when she extended to him her hand, she felt flustered, an emotion caused by her vivid memory of the kiss in the theater the night before. Don Rafael left them for a few minutes to finish an urgent letter he had begun. The two young people, seated in rocking chairs, fell into the eternal conversation of lovers, into that blissful talk of low voices in which the words meant nothing but the eyes said everything.

"I thought you were going to come back here with us this morning, but you must have forgotten," she said.

"It wasn't possible. At five this morning friends awoke me with a serenade, and I was with them until seven. Tomorrow night they'll throw a banquet for me at the Hotel Washington."

"What are the newspapers saying about the premiere?"

"I brought them with me. Their comments are long and their praise is exaggerated. Today I was almost embarrassed to go outside."

Margarita anxiously thumbed through the papers, and scanning the reviews her face flushed with satisfaction. She felt very pleased with his success. After all, the artist praised by the public was hers, exclusively hers. She felt both like crying and laughing, an extension of the passion that overcame her the night before. Finally her real feelings poured from her lips, to the delight of Fernando.

"Listen," she whispered, "I never thought I would ever love anyone the way I love you. Last night I couldn't sleep thinking that you might have gone out to dinner with those actresses. I want to have you with me always, forever. I don't want you to even glance at anyone but me. I don't want you to even talk to anyone else. Sometimes I'm even jealous of your writing because I feel it keeps you away from me."

He listened attentively to those unexpected words. They didn't seem real. Could his ears be deceiving him?

When he spoke, he too expressed his own emotion, no less ardently than she had. For him, without parents or brothers and sisters, Margarita was everything: hope, dreams, ideals. Never could he love another woman. A heart like his, once consumed with emotion, never recovered.

A long, unpleasant sound broke the spell. It was Mr. Ward, who had just pulled up in his automobile. He exclaimed with satisfaction, "I finally made it here in my car. If I couldn't have gotten over that ridge this time, I think I would have hired an army of workers to flatten the road."

The lovers looked at each other with that resignation of those obliged to put up with an intruder. But their annoyance was brief because Don Rafael promptly escorted the foreigner into his office in order to show him plans for some improvements he intended to make on the estate.

The blond young man with Napoleonic features, intelligent, well educated, of few words, with excellent business sense had won the respect and affection of the old man. If he enjoyed discussing his favorite literature with Fernando, he recognized the superiority of the American in matters of science, business, and statistics. He had often thought to himself, "What a pity that in this world no one is perfect. If we could just combine those two young men into one!"

At noon everyone sat down at the dining room table, arranged with impeccable taste and regally served. Don Rafael had gone all out, as was his habit when he hosted people he loved. They spent a couple of delightful hours at the table enjoying the rich food, select wines, and good humor of all and in particular of Doña Virginia.

After finishing the meal, the men retired to the garden to smoke, while the two women hosted some friends from a neighboring estate in the living room. While enjoying the fresh air and smoking excellent Havanas, Don Rafael and his guests leafed through the newspapers and commented on the reviews.

"The press," Mr. Ward began directing his words to Fernando, "has given as much attention to the moral of your drama as it did to the literary qualities. The audience applauded your work enthusiastically last night but didn't seem to heed the lesson you wanted to give them. At Tuesday night's performance we'll see the same show of luxury, the same vain and immoral ostentation on the part of people who wouldn't stop at committing a crime in order not to appear impoverished."

"I'm convinced," the poet replied, "that the theater is incapable of eliminating the vices of society. It's nothing more than the reflection of the customs of the period. Still, I'm also sure that denouncing them focuses the attention of sensitive and patriotic people on them and prompts them to set about correcting those vices."

Don Rafael gravely observed, "The task of Fernando couldn't be nobler and better intended. He wants to correct injustices, and in doing so, just like Don Quixote, he reaps a harvest of abuse."

"I understand all that," the lawyer replied, "and far from discouraging me it only serves to strengthen my resolve. During those years I was away from my country my love for it increased. I wouldn't consider myself worthy of my country if I didn't try to contribute to its well being with the few talents I have."

After a pause, Don Rafael spoke up, "The truth is that the Costa Ricans have lost many of their former virtues. They used to have more respect for the property of others; they entrusted couriers with considerable sums of money that arrived at their destination without one cent missing; the idle were regarded as criminals. Today just the opposite is true. It's hard to find an honest worker. Robbery and murder multiply at an alarming rate. The unemployed fill the streets of the cities, while the fields remain unattended; misery is commonplace; and the numbers of drunks and prostitutes are frightening."

Mr. Ward broke in, "I've only lived in Costa Rica

about two years but I've lived in other countries in Central America and my observations concur with those of Don Rafael. Those who've never traveled are not able to perceive the defects and absurdities of their country as well as a foreigner can. These natives are like passengers on a train who can't appreciate the speed without looking out the window."

"Wait a minute," Señor Montalvo interjected. "We know and we confess our vices which are neither as many nor as great as in other nations. Those that we have are imported from abroad as a part of what is called progress, and I tell you that we lived very well for a long time without that wretched progress which has been more of a curse than a blessing. In spite of our problems, I believe that our country can still be among the most moral and industrious in the world."

At that moment, a servant interrupted to inform Don Rafael that someone had arrived to see him, and the two young men were left alone.

"I'm pleased," said the Yankee, "to be able to speak of these matters with a person as highly educated as you without exciting the chauvinism of Señor Montalvo. I guess in my own country we are frank to the point of rudeness, and I would like to be frank with you if you'll permit me."

"And why not?"

"O.K., then, the evil is even greater than you yourself imagine. I've traveled throughout a good part of this country visiting farms, factories, offices, and schools; I've read in the National Library the collections of magazines and in the National Archives the historical documents; I've lived in both the countryside and the city. In short, I take pride in knowing this republic better than most, better than the majority of its inhabitants. Are you surprised?" he added smiling at Fernando's wide-eyed gaze. "Don't mistake me for a foreign agent or spy. I work only for myself. These unexploited regions offer great opportunities for my race, and with our initiative they will become in time the sites of vast industrial enterprises. What is strange about the Americans wanting to get to know well the regions of our future business expansion?" He was speaking in English, a language Fernando knew well, but he expressed himself with unusual ardor, almost as if the champagne served at lunch had loosened his tongue. He continued, "Alcohol undermines these people. We North Americans are famous as drinkers, but comparing statistics and taking into account the enormous quantity of illegal liquor that is consumed here, I assure you that in your country people drink, in proportion, four times more than they do in mine. I attended the celebrations of the national holiday in the capital last year, and I couldn't stand the smell of aguardiente that pervaded the streets. On Sunday I went to a village to hire some workers, and everyone was drunk. In the countryside all the festivities end in drunken brawls. The degenerate children. . . ."

"Wait just a moment," interrupted Fernando. "The people shouldn't be blamed; rather it is the fault of the government that won't close down the National Liquor Factory."

"And why don't the municipal governments, the journalists, the teachers, and other patriots who should look after the public well-being protest?"

I've written various articles on that subject," responded Fernando, "but don't fool yourself, nothing can be done until the people themselves understand the danger."

"The people! The people!" Mr. Ward exclaimed with disdain. "The people don't advance unless they're pulled from above, from the ruling class, from the educated class. The people are as unconscious as children, as unconscious as this tree," the Yankee continued striking the huge fig tree with his ample hand, "which needs the care of a gardener if it is to avoid being devoured by parasites. Just look at this," he said rising suddenly.

Fernando approached the trunk to look at the place

where the American was pointing with a finger. He saw a long, wide fissure in the depths of one of the grooves whose blackness contrasted with the leaden color of the bark.

"This tree," said Mr. Ward, "is beginning to rot. If it isn't cured in time it will die. I pointed this out to Don Rafael the other day and he became furious. He won't tolerate anyone who indicates the defects of his *son*. And to think that it could be cured with a little tar! Do you understand? Tar!" he emphasized with an ironic smile.

The sky suddenly had become overcast and the winds brought to the garden a cold drizzle which worsened with each passing minute. Both men walked silently back to the house, the one serene and smiling, the other pensive and perturbed.

V

The Hunt

I F THE HOMAGE the public paid the poet on the opening night of his drama was memorable, the enthusiasm displayed when the play was repeated on Tuesday was nothing short of delirious. In fact, the National Theater never had witnessed a similar display. Margarita would have been beside herself with joy if she had been present at the new triumph of her lover. A torrential rainstorm turned the road into a quagmire, making it impossible for the family to attend the second performance. Don Rafael telegraphed Fernando that afternoon from San Isidro expressing his regrets.

On Wednesday, the lawyer received a long and affectionate letter from his loved one and another from Señor Montalvo inviting him to take part in a hunt on the following Sunday. He suggested that Fernando plan to spend Saturday night with them so that they could get an early start in the morning and informed him that Mr. Ward also had been invited to participate, partly because the American often had expressed his enthusiasm for that sport and partly so that Fernando would have a young companion for the hunt.

The poet showed scant enthusiasm for that companionship. Without being able to explain why, he found the Yankee increasingly burdensome. Was it perhaps because of racial prejudice, the difference of character and ideals, or the superiority the American displayed in his words and manner when he dealt with Latin peoples? Of course, any expert in matters of the heart might regard such dislike as the natural distrust or, perhaps more properly put, jealousy, of a man who sees interposed between himself and his beloved an outsider, particularly if he is a handsome, intelligent bachelor. It is true up to that point Fernando had never witnessed in Mr. Ward the slightest sign of interest in the young lady. In fact, he rarely paid any attention to her. For her part, Margarita only had eyes for her poet. One thing, however, greatly disturbed our hero: the definite predilection Don Rafael showed for the foreigner. They shared similar tastes, hobbies, and temperaments.

With those misgivings, Fernando arrived at El Higuerón Saturday afternoon. There was one other reason for his bad humor. On the previous day, an anonymous article appeared in the newspaper *La Información* which, for the first time, contained some unfavorable comments about his play. The unknown critic termed it immoral and absurd, attributing the triumph of the playwright not to his talent but to the fact that he was one of the prestigious leaders of the Progressive Party. Since that party was composed largely of artisans and farmers it seemed obvious—at least to the anonymous critic—that the play had been written with the political goal of pleasing the political passions of the people.

Fernando found Mr. Ward already there. He had arrived just a half-hour earlier on a handsome horse and carried a magnificent double-barreled shotgun.

The troublesome newspaper article became the immediate topic of conversation. It had aroused the indignation of all present. Don Rafael used bitter invectives against the envidious writer; Margarita cried from anger; and even Doña Virginia, losing her customary equanimity, bitterly criticized the anonymous coward. That wonderful woman loved Fernando like a son and of all the many suitors of her niece only he had won her support from the start. When the conversation quieted down, Mr. Ward said to Fernando, "That was only to be expected and I didn't want to say anything to you before so as not to dampen your success with my pessimism. In other countries, they value and support those who struggle to rise above the ordinary, but here. . . ."

"Don't go on," interrupted Don Rafael, unable to contain himself. "How can you judge all of us by the pettiness of one? Costa Ricans know how to appreciate what is worthwhile and we take pride in the triumphs of one of our own."

The Yankee opened his mouth to reply but what he was about to say doubtless seemed inopportune to him or perhaps too strong. Instead of words an enigmatic smile formed on his lips.

During dinner Don Rafael explained the plan for the hunt the next day. They would leave at dawn for the mountainous country he owned near the Irazú Volcano where wild game abounded, above all, deer and sainos and even some pumas and jaguars. They would take Fermín as a guide. He owned a couple of dogs that loved to hunt. The ladies would accompany the hunters as far as the camp site where they would remain with Don Rafael whose age no longer permitted him to tramp through the forest.

Before going to bed, Fernando had an opportunity to talk with his adored Margarita at one end of the living room. As it turned out, that ill-fated day didn't end without one more frustration, this one caused by an innocent remark of Margarita.

"Haven't you noticed," she unexpectedly observed, "what a penetrating look Mr. Ward has? When he looks at me, I turn beet red, and I feel that he can read my most hidden thoughts."

"I hadn't noticed," Fernando responded coolly. He became very serious and looked away for a long time.

"What's the matter?" Margarita finally asked, aware of the sudden change in her lover.

"Nothing," he dryly replied.

Such unaccustomed hardness stunned the young woman. Disturbed and anxious she repeated her question several times. She spoke affectionately to him, but when she continued to encounter coldness she began to cry quietly. Those tears convinced Fernando that his jealousy had caused him to act ridiculously. He asked her pardon and taking advantage of a brief moment when Doña Virginia turned her back to close a window, he kissed the tears on the cheeks of his lover.

Just before sunrise, the mounted procession left the farm in this order: in the lead Don Rafael with Fermín preceded by the dogs and a mule loaded with provisions; then Mr. Ward and Doña Virginia on their horses; then Fernando on his Manelik and Margarita on a prancing young horse whose spirited temper disturbed Don Rafael. He made his daughter bring up the rear of the procession for fear that the animal might run away. Margarita was as happy and talkative as a schoolgirl on vacation. The penetrating cold of those altitudes turned her cheeks pink and beneath the brim of her felt hat her brown eyes sparkled. "Shall we scare Dad and gallop past him? Look at Mother flirting with Mr. Ward! Are you becoming serious again? O.K., I'm going to keep quiet."

Fernando smiled as he listened to her. He gazed at her lovely features, her full and well-shaped breasts, and the tiny foot that appeared beneath the folds of her blue skirt. From time to time, he put his hand on the neck of her white horse as if to control it but instead of grabbing the reins he squeezed the hand that held them. "Careful! They'll see you," she stammered.

The rising sun scattered one after the other the light clouds hanging over the valley. Soon the central plateau stood out clearly in all its richness and abundance before the gaze of the travelers. In the excitement of witnessing that beautiful scene below, Margarita named all the villages that began to appear in the foothills of the mountains as if they had been awakened by dawn's light. The riders paused frequently to enjoy the landscape whose dimensions widened as they climbed until they lost sight of the valley when they entered the narrow path of the forest. After an hour of that difficult path they came upon a clearing covered with grass still whitened by frost. Nearby ran a noisy stream of clear water. Don Rafael dismounted and spoke, "We'll have lunch here after you return from your hunt. The forest is too thick for the horses. Leave them here. Don't worry. Fermín knows this region well and with him there's no danger of getting lost. I'll stay here with the ladies."

The overseer tied the horses to some trees, unloaded the mule, and throwing his old gun over his shoulder he then whistled for the dogs. He led the way into the thicket cutting a path with his machete. The two hunters followed. Don Rafael and his family had a thousand pieces of last minute advice to give. Then the old man, exhausted by the three-hour climb, went to stretch out along the stream. Aunt and niece busied themselves unloading the baskets and spreading the contents on the grass.

A half hour had not passed before they heard the dogs barking in the distance, followed by two shots. "Ah, they've found something!" exclaimed Don Rafael with obvious satisfaction. Another half hour passed and the barking could be heard again. A single shot sounded faintly. Then, for a long time, neither the dogs nor the guns could be heard.

"Do you think something might have happened?" a nervous Margarita asked.

"They'll be back shortly," replied Don Rafael, "and

they won't be empty handed."

Soon thereafter the machete of Fermín could be heard nearby, on the opposite side of the clearing from where they'd left. Ten minutes later the two hunters appeared shouting with joy. The American carried over his shoulder a fat peccary and Fermín had a mountain goat that Fernando had shot. Don Rafael opposed the idea of his overseer to skin the animals and ordered them put on the mule to be taken back to the estate as trophys.

Lunch was delicious and among the savory dishes that appeared from the baskets special praise went to the chicken tamales prepared by the skilled hands of Doña Virginia. After everyone had drunk the coffee Margarita had heated on the portable alcohol stove, the two lovers went to sit on one of the boulders along the bed of the stream, while the other excursionists sat in a group on the grass.

Some noisy squawkings suddenly attracted everyone's attention, especially Fermín's who was busily loading the game on the mule.

"What was that?" questioned Margarita.

"They're turkeys," the farmer answered. "And they're close by."

"Can you believe that I've never seen turkeys even though I've lived in the country for such a long time," Margarita confided to her lover.

"Well, then, I'll bring you one," he answered. Fernando rose and picked up his gun.

"Don't be silly. I don't want you to go."

"It'll only take a few minutes. Come on, Fermín."

Fermín eagerly accepted the invitation. He tied up the dogs so that they wouldn't scare the turkeys and shouldered his old gun, which he wouldn't have exchanged for the expensive shotgun of Mr. Ward. He led the way into the forest, followed by Fernando.

Margarita remained in her same place without taking part in the general conversation. She understood that Fernando didn't appreciate her exchanging words or looks with the foreigner and didn't want to cause him even the slightest annoyance.

Although it was a little past mid-day, the coolness increased because the dense fog that enveloped the mountain shut out the sun's rays. The horses nibbled at the grass within their reach. The two dogs slept soundly.

Mr. Ward entertained his friends with some tales of his adventures in Colombia that all, including Margarita, listened to with interest, when a slight rustle of the bushes but a few feet away caught their attention. Turning toward it, they sighted a strange animal, somewhat like a boar, which, as surprised as they were, stood frozen. Then, trying to run away, it had the bad luck of becoming entangled in some vines.

"A baby tapir! A baby tapir!" Don Rafael shouted excitedly. Mr. Ward jumped up and ran to capture the little creature that struggled without success to free itself. The little animal let out a kind of whistle answered by an impressive grunt, something like a trumpet sound from close by. Dry branches cracked, the bushes parted, an enormus tapir emerged like a hurricane, its eyes aflame and its rage vented through furious panting. This herbivorous animal, ordinarily very timid, becomes formidable when it defends its young and with the same ease its muscular chest opens a path through the densest undergrowth of the forests it can knock down and trample any hunter who tries to harm its offspring.

Margarita, filled with fear, ran to embrace Doña Virginia; Don Rafael stood in front of them to protect them with his body; and Mr. Ward without any time to pick up his shotgun, reached for the pistol in his belt. The beast attacked with the speed of light but the Yankee, sidestepping the charge, fired two shots from his automatic pistol into the animal's head. The tapir jumped, staggered to a halt, and fell with a heavy thud almost at the feet of Don Rafael, while the baby, free at last from its imprisonment, scampered off into the woods.

Doña Virginia, pale but serene, comforted her niece who had fainted. Señor Montalvo hunted among the provisions for the bottle of cognac. Mr. Ward quietly put away his pistol and then filled a glass of water from the stream for Margarita. At that precise moment two nearly simultaneous shots resounded in the distance.

A quarter of an hour later, after Margarita had calmed down, they laughed together about their adventure and fright while they examined the strange animal. It was in that state that Fernando and the overseer found them when they returned with the turkeys. Upon viewing that scene and in particular the signs of terror in the eyes of his beloved, Fernando stopped surprised. In a few words, Don Rafael explained what had happened, not without praising the calmness of the American and his immediate response to the danger.

The hunters had wanted to take the dead tapir back with them, but Fermín had objected, pointing out that the mule couldn't carry everything. They agreed that he would stay to skin the huge tapir, while the others returned to the hacienda.

Once back at the house, Don Rafael insisted that his guests have a cup of tea before returning to the city. Both accepted. On leaving the table, Mr. Ward spoke, "Don Rafael, on Thursday, the 11th of April, there will be a soccer game at the Sabana between the teams of San José and Puerto Limón of which I am the captain. In the name of my friends, I invite all of you to the game and I specially request the honor of having the young lady distribute the medals which the legation of my country will confer on the victors."

Before Margarita could open her mouth, her father replied, "I thank you and of course I accept the invitation as well as the honor you bestow on my daughter."

Margarita tried to protest, looking questioningly at her boyfriend. Standing by his side, she said in a low voice so that only he could hear, "I won't be going."

"What not?" he asked in the same tone. She turned to look closely at him in order to understand his attitude. When they took leave of each other, she asked, "Do you really want me to go?"

"Of course. It'll be a wonderful opportunity for us to spend another day together."

After the two young men left, Margarita remained standing on the porch. She watched the two riders as they disappeared behind clouds of dust in the direction of San Isidro.

VI

The Playing Field

ATHOUGH WOMEN may profess some special insight into romantic affairs, Margarita was unable to explain the insistence of her fiancée that she preside over the soccer match. Hadn't he become annoyed the day before the hunt over a simple observation she had made about the penetrating look of the American? How was it then on the following day instead of being disgusted by the American's invitation, he had urged her to accept it? She was far from suspecting the motives for that seemingly contradictory behavior. A suspicion as vague as those vapors that rise from rivers in the early morning had hovered in the mind of the poet.

"Jealousy," observed Doña Virginia, "is like the barbs of the prickly pear: They are small but can cause great discomfort; they can't be extracted with pincers but only come out when they want to." A similar barb pricked Fernando: the words of his beloved, the frequent visits of the foreigner with the motive or perhaps the pretext of conducting business, and certain furtive glances that he believed he saw them exchange. He sought an occasion to either prove or disprove his suspicion, and he thought the game might provide just the occasion.

He had one of those emotional temperaments, characteristic of artists, in which sentiment ruled absolutely, sometimes offering them pleasures denied to other mortals, other times driving them to excesses and to violence. Education often inhibited those temperaments to some degree and self-control sometimes hid them behind a mask of seeming indifference. But similar to volcanos dormant for long centuries and shrouded in dust, those temperaments only need a fire within to produce catastrophic results.

Could it be true that the foreigner had taken a fancy for Margarita? Could it possibly be true that she'd forgotten her promises and her recent demonstrations of love? Although such questions might seem absurd, they tormented Fernando during the days preceding the game when he hoped to resolve once and for all his lingering doubts.

The people of the capital displayed great enthusiasm for that exotic game that had replaced national sports in all the Latin American countries. It synthesized the Anglo-Saxon character, its cult of health and physical beauty and its partiality for sports that required strength and courage. The event assumed even greater importance because it took place on the national holiday, the anniversary of the defeat of the North American adventurers by the Costa Ricans at Rivas in 1856. On the same day their ancestors once met in battle, the descendants would meet on the playing field.

Starting at seven in the morning, the crowds began to converge on Sabana Park in coaches, automobiles and streetcars, and those who couldn't afford the high prices of transportation walked. The expansive Sabana, whose uniform surface resembled a green lake, suggested the theory that it had been created by the Indians in pre-Columbian times to perform who knows what strange religious ceremonies. On that morning the fields seemed to undulate with the coming and going of thousands of people. In the rows of seats surrounding the playing field, the silk parasols gave the appearance of rows of bright flowers, while a living border, formed almost in its entirety by little children, surrounded the field marked off by Costa Rican and North American flags. At nine on the dot, Don Rafael and his family arrived in the automobile that Mr. Ward gallantly had put at their disposal.

The queen of the festivities was dazzling: She wore a low-cut gown of blue velvet; from her well sculptured neck hung a diamond necklace, and in her delicately shaped arms rested a large spray of white lilies. Her eyes more brilliant than ever sought anxiously for Fernando, but the lawyer didn't arrive until the precise moment when the whistle sounded to begin the game. After greeting his many friends, he sat down at Margarita's side. The whistle sounded again. From the tents put up at both ends of the playing field the two teams, the Americans in blue and the Costa Ricans in red, filed onto the field.

The American team was composed of a magnificent group of athletes, while the Coast Ricans displayed a great variety of heights, complexions, and even colors. More than anyone else, Mr. Ward was the object of the spectators' admiration. In truth, it would be necessary to refer back to classical statuary to find a model of such an admirable combination of strength and beauty, of so much elegance and naturalness in attitude and movement. After each player took his place, the game began. From the beginning the superiority of the foreigners was apparent. They played as a team, displaying incomparable skill and strength.

All eyes focused on Mr. Ward. It was the first time he had played in the capital. The presence of the formidable adversary rattled the local team a bit. The first goal came quickly enough. The captain of the American team, kicking the ball in front of him, evaded those who tried to take it away from him and then with a strong, sure kick sent the ball flying into the net for a goal. The crowd wildly applauded that skill. In the second quarter, the Costa Ricans played their best but it wasn't good enough. Mr. Ward had the honor of making two more goals, one right after the other. The enthusiasm of the crowd reached a crescendo. Margarita jumped to her feet as did most of the spectators. She attentively followed the plays of the game without noting the severe and disdainful expression on Fernando's face.

The national team fought heroically in the third quarter but suffered the same bad luck as they had in the previous ones. That devil of a Yankee was invincible. Always agile, strong, without showing the slightest sign of fatigue, he alone could defeat the opposing team. He seemed determined not even to let his teammates outshine him. He continued to make some spectacular plays and for the fourth time he sent the ball into the net with the same precision with which a mortar might launch a grenade. Amid deafening applause and frantic hurrays, the crowd streamed onto the playing field to carry the victor in triumph to the presidential box to receive the prize.

Margarita's hand trembled as she pinned the medal of gold on his chest. Her face seemed somewhat pale and she kept her eyes lowered, details that did not escape Fernando's attention. After his companions also had received their medals, Mr. Ward said to Don Rafael, "I hope you and Mr. Rodríguez will honor me by stopping by my house. The auto is ready to take us there." There was nothing to do but accept, and as soon as the Yankee had changed clothes, they left for his handsome mansion, which he recently had acquired in the suburb of Otoya.

On the way, Don Rafael mused, "Doesn't it seem to you a bit ironic that on this festive day when we celebrate the defeat of the Americans on April 11, 1856, they've turned the tables today and defeated the Costa Ricans?"

"It's very just," Mr. Ward answered with a smile,

"that after half a century we get our revenge."

"Oh, there's a slight difference," observed Doña Virginia mischievously. "You defeated the *ticos* with leather balls; they defeated you with leaden ones."

The residence of the American greatly impressed his guests. It was decorated with that practical luxury of the Anglo-Saxons, a combination of beauty and utility without crowding the rooms with those objects, more a hindrance than a need, with which pretentious people make a show of wealth and elegance. The meal was no less impressive. Well-trained foreign servants served it to the accompaniment of pleasant background music.

Over dessert, a heated discussion took place about the principal causes for the defeat of the San José team. With his national pride obviously wounded, Don Rafael tried to show that the Americans owed their victory exclusively to greater practice and more careful training.

"It's true," Mr. Ward responded gravely, "that preparation is more fundamental than you imagine. It is a tradition of our race. Conscious of its mission, my people have always educated themselves for an active life. To struggle with nature, to conquer it, and to extract from it all its treasure from which all mankind will benefit. For that reason, we are concerned with creating healthy, strong, brave, and enterprising youth, while the other races, still infected with influences spread through Europe by the Arabs, are preoccupied with dreams, mysticism, and poetry, condemning themselves inevitably to genocide."

Fernando, feeling that those remarks alluded to him, immediately answered, "Without denying that practical education is the basis for the prosperity of the United States, one also must confess that it is too *terre a terre,* as the French say, because it forgets that the soul doesn't live by bread alone. It is also necessary to satisfy higher longings."

Without being able to supress a feeling of impatience,

Mr. Ward argued, "And who says that we disdain what you call higher culture and do not render homage to the arts? The thing is that we begin at the beginning. We clear the forests and live in huts until the land produces; after sufficient harvests, we build a house; when we have earned money, we surround ourselves with comforts; and finally when we no longer need to devote all our time to work, we have the leisure to enjoy the arts, that is to say, we can devote time to the spirit. To the contrary, in various Latin American countries that I know and whose natural riches are prodigious the youth rejects anything requiring effort, looks with disgust on agriculture and industry, and dissipates the best years in literary leisure, writing verses, articles, and speeches as if the larger the number of poets and orators the greater will be the nation's prosperity. So long as the young people trod the pleasant if sterile path of these pastimes instead of following the more difficult path of hard work, it is useless to even think about progress."

"I suppose you count our country as one of those whose young people prefer leisure to hard work," Don Rafael volunteered somewhat uncomfortably.

"I hope you won't take offense at what I'm about to say. Here there has been no thought given to reforming education as there was in Germany when they discovered that despite their philosophers and poets they were falling behind, or as in Japan where they adopted European culture to avoid being overpowered. I've visited quite a few schools in this Republic and never did I see a model of an airplane, of a submarine, or of other modern machines that everyone should know something about. Not one student knew what magnesium was or what its uses were despite the fact that a day doesn't pass when new discoveries of that substance are made. I don't remember in which of those schools I visited that the students spent the entire year discussing Egyptian and Greek metaphysics but didn't know the names of renowned modern chemists, biologists, and astronomers. If I were a Costa Rican and a journalist, I would spend all my time denouncing these absurdities. As a foreigner, I simply point them out in private, because I believe that the best proof of affection that can be given a friend is to tell the truth. That's exactly why I applaud the work of Fernando, who is one of the very few with no fear of prescribing bitter medicine to the nation so that it can recover its good health." The Yankee spoke with unusual ardor as if he felt the excitement of the game and the joy of victory.

Fernando listened with total attention: Don Rafael was visibly mortified; Margarita kept her eyes lowered; and Doña Virginia displayed her eternal but enigmatic smile. The host understood that perhaps he had gone too far and hastened to soften his criticism with these words, "The one who wrote *At the Edge of the Abyss* knows how to portray in a masterful manner the vices of a society and will find the ways of correcting them for the good of this delightful country. I propose that we honor that poet with another glass of champagne."

Once in the street Don Rafael said to Fernando, "When that man comes to see me again, I'm going to give him a piece of my mind and show him how mistaken he is. What did you think of those rude remarks he made?"

Sadly lowering his head, Fernando murmured, "He spoke the truth."

 VII

Politics

ACCORDING TO THE MUCH abused expression of the press at that time, ominous clouds hung over the political horizon, fortelling a frightening storm. Nothing stirred the Latin Americans more than politics, not so much the politics oriented by grand ideals and vital interests as those of the parochial spirit, personalism, and intrigue. The people attracted to such politics sought in the triumph of such and such a party their own profit, their own well being, or at least some crumbs from the political banquet table.

Elections were slated for the third week of April but for three months the political cauldron of the country bubbled, heated by the constant propaganda of the parties and by the frequent clashes that occurred among the partisans. The official candidate for the presidency, a distinguished lawyer, ran against an impressive adversary, also a lawyer (men of the courts enjoy among us a divine right to monopolize public administration). The opposition counted on its side the majority of the people, and in order to defeat it the government needed to put into play all the tricks, schemes, and arbitrariness customary on such occasions.

Fernando participated in the ranks of the opposition and with him the cream of the youth of San José. According to some gossip, his political affiliation accounted for some of the noisy success his first drama had enjoyed. His name figured among the editors of the *Herald,* the newspaper of the Progressive Party, where his well-written and thoughtful articles did more for the party's cause than all the patriotic speeches of the party hacks. His law office served as the headquarters of the leaders of the opposition. He left the daily business of the courts and the law in the hands of his assistants who dealt with those more mundane details.

Busy as he was, Fernando did not neglect his weekly visits to the countryside. By a happy coincidence, Don Rafael decided to spend a short time in the capital in order to oversee some repairs he intended to make in his city house located in the suburb of Amon. The young man took advantage of that opportunity to see his fiancée daily.

Margarita seemed to be more in love than ever. Fearful of displeasing her sweetheart, whose jealous nature had become evident on many occasions, she went out very little, didn't attend the theater, and hardly was seen by anyone. She treated visitors, and especially Mr. Ward, in a reserved manner, knowing that the American's regular attention annoyed Fernando. Indeed, the presence of the foreigner aroused in her mixed emotions, a combination of shyness and fear. Before his cool, scrutinizing eyes that, as she said, seemed to penetrate to the depths of her soul, she felt like a criminal before a judge or a student in the presence of a severe and inflexible teacher. Her own lack of strength annoyed her, and she promised herself not to be intimidated by the looks of the Yankee on his next visit, but when again she found herself in front of him, her resolution vanished and she again felt that inexplicable confusion. Perhaps it might be said that her fragile, unpredictable, and excessively sensitive nature felt subjected to the powerful suggestion of that audacious, handsome, and intelligent man who seemed to know neither danger nor inhibitions. Had Fernando understood this phenomenon? It is impossible that such things pass unnoticed by those in love; indeed, that tension and uncertainty probably fed the lively jealousy that Fernando exhibited, a jealousy that made a martyr of Margarita. He interpreted the tension as a secret passion, perhaps even as a manifestation of love born out of the famous victory of the American on the playing field of the Sabana, which he felt must have made a deep impression on the feelings of the young woman.

Jealousy haunted Fernando. Would it be possible that his beloved and the rest of society for that matter valued an athletic victory more than they did a contribution to the arts? Wouldn't it be a sure sign of barbarity to favor brute force over talent, the muscle over the brain, the material over the spirit? In his conversations with Margarita, he found opportunities to make allusions to what he considered to be childish pastimes, unworthy of serious men, and to the slight enthusiasm the Costa Rican youth showed for exotic and imported games that seemed part of a fad and nothing more.

Señor Montalvo shared his views. He compared those sports intended for the recreation of school children with the great national sport, bullfighting, in which the participants displayed fearless courage and even a contempt of death, qualities characteristic of the Hispanic race. Fernando didn't contradict the old man even though he disliked that bloody sport, too. Still, he was pleased to hear Don Rafael disdain soccer because his condemnation helped to ease the pain of the victory of the North Americans in that disastrous game with the Costa Ricans.

Meanwhile, political activities had reached a boiling point, the cauldron of intrigue bubbled furiously. All signs indicated that the official candidate would go down in a humiliating defeat. The government vainly drew from its inexhaustable arsenal of resources to win the campaign. In

the primaries neither bribes nor threats nor tricks helped
the government's cause. The opposition received an impressive majority of the votes. Consequently Fernando
was certain of a seat in the Chamber of Deputies; he might
even become a minister.

Alienated from politics by temperament and habit,
Don Rafael tried vainly to dampen the ardor of his young
friend and persuade him to abandon the dangerous career
of politics. Margarita shared that, but she exerted no more
influence over Fernando in that regard than her father did.
In fact, the ineffectiveness of her pleas annoyed her. Fernando was ready to run the same risks as the others in his
party, and it was too late to turn back without damaging
his reputation and ideals.

To assure its success, the government had no alter-
native but to abandon scruples and take the inevitable
measures to win. One night several days after the voting,
Fernando was visiting his fiancée's house when a neighbor
arrived with the news that the government had suspended
individual guarantees and arrested the winning presidential candidate as well as several prominent members of his
party. The bearer of that news, an old merchant who
never participated in any elections, had seen with his own
eyes the squadrons of soldiers in the street and the
detachments of policemen making arrests. That news profoundly disturbed the household. Everyone looked at Fernando with questioning eyes. He prepared to leave at
once.

"Where will you go?" a pale Margarita asked.

"It wouldn't be wise to leave now," observed Doña
Virginia. "Surely they're looking for you, and it would be
better to hide here."

"No," objected Don Rafael. "They're certain to come
search this house. It would be better to go to the country
house and stay there until this political storm passes over.
Look, go out the back way, take my horse, and leave town
by way of San Francisco."

"I appreciate your concern, but I can't hide and I can't flee. I must stand with my friends. We celebrated our victory together, and I feel I must share this setback with them. There's no reason for fear," he continued quietly, disturbed by the anxious look on Margarita's face. "All it means is that we'll be locked up for a week while the government uses bayonets instead of ballots to proclaim its electoral victory. The public will accept events without complaint as they always have in the past. When the government is convinced that it has overreacted against a peaceful party like ours, it will relent and set us free. . . ."

To the other arguments his friends used to try to dissuade him, Fernando invariably gave the same response: He refused to flee. While leaving, he was able to whisper to Margarita while Don Rafael stood in the street outside the door to see if anything was happening, "If luck has it that we might be separated for a long time, will you think of me everyday?"

"Every minute, every second," she answered.

Then he embraced her passionately, kissing her eyes and mouth with feverish emotion. Don Rafael remained standing at his door until the young man had turned the corner. The streets were deserted and the houses quiet, but near his own house Fernando ran into a police detachment armed to the teeth. They arrested him and led him to headquarters. Under heavy guard, they moved him to the Atlantic coast. On the following day, when the public became aware of the scandalous arrests and behavior of the government, the prisoners already had been put aboard a ship in Puerto Limón destined for exile in the United States. The officials did not permit them to speak with anyone, nor even to write their families.

The events gravely upset Don Rafael; the indifference of his fellow citizens toward the flagrant violation of the law annoyed him. He decided to return to his country estate not only to escape the oppressive atmosphere of the capital but principally to see if the fresh air might help counteract the depression Margarita suffered because of the political events that weighted so heavily on her personal life and happiness.

VIII

Exile

MY BELOVED, they say that the heart is never wrong, and I agree, because mine suspected that the last time we saw each other that we would be separated for a long time. If the land feels lonely after the sun sets, it at least has the consolation that the sun will return the next day. I have no such consolation. I do not know when I will see you again. I do not know when my sun will shine again to relieve my sadness and loneliness. When you were here, I spent the week counting the days until Sunday. Imagine how it is now! Imagine how cruel and eternal are the hours now that I have no hope of seeing you. We are at El Higuerón because the doctor believes that in the country I'll get better without understanding that I'll die here sooner because in every corner of this house there is a memory of you. Alone where we were once together, I cry without being able to stop. Papa scolds me sometimes; he tries to amuse me with excursions, and he's even taken me to some parties and dances. Mama Virginia tries to console me by talking about you and assuring me that your exile will not last for long. The old woman loves you very much. Instead of being jealous, I find myself loving her more because she loves *you so much. How silly I am! You should know that many nights I wake up terrified, imagining that you have abandoned me for one of those horrible New York girls. They are such flirts and so fresh! If you have forgotten me, please don't tell me because I will do something terrible to make you regret your forgetfulness the rest of your life. Ah, you see how ugly I can be! Perhaps more so than before, but your absence is to blame. How could you get involved in politics instead of spending your time with me? Please write me twice a day so that I am certain of receiving a letter from you each time the mail arrives. I send you all my love, all my heart and soul, and if you are behaving well I send you one of the many kisses I save for you. Your Margarita.*

Isolated in the luxurious rooms of the Hotel Astoria, where his three companions in exile also stayed, Fernando read and reread the letter whose words of passion resounded throughout his soul like the sweetest of music. Accompanying the letter from Margarita was a long one from Don Rafael and another from Doña Virginia.

Don Rafael informed him that he had colosed the land deal with Mr. Ward, selling him the estate in Nicoya for seventy thousand dollars. He spoke confidentially of how several influential friends had tried to get an amnesty for the exiles and showed his indignation with some of the politicians who had opposed the government but with incredible cynicism had accepted important positions in it.

Doña Virginia, after some sly remarks about the current political situation, gave a minute account of the daily events of the family at El Higuerón and spoke of the almost daily visits of Mr. Ward who had become extremely close to Don Rafael. The old man was very enthusiastic about the installation of an electrical generator on the farm in order to establish a cheese factory equal or perhaps superior to the foreign ones and a milk processing plant that would be a model in all respects. The idea of the Yankee spending all his time at the estate of Don Rafael didn't please Fernando and put him into a bad mood for the remainder of the day. The maid found him in that frame of mind when she announced the visit of two gentlemen whose names, elegantly printed on two cards, were completely unknown to him:

HENRY WARD
Manager of the Ottawa Bank

JOHN SWEET
President of the C.A. Mining Co.

These two gentlemen explained their mission. That very morning they had received letters from their common friend, Thomas Ward, requesting them to inquire from the Costa Rican consulate the whereabouts of Don Fernando Rodríguez in order to offer their services, to help solve any difficulties that he might encounter, to acquaint him with New York, and to do whatever possible to make his stay in that city as pleasant as possible.

Not withstanding the instinctive dislike that Mr. Ward inspired in him, Fernando couldn't help but appreciate that generous gesture. He expressed his gratitude in a letter to him the following day, although in his correspondence with the Montalvo family he didn't even mention the matter.

He rarely took part in the excursions and travels with which the presidential candidate and the other two exiles amused themselves, but his new acquaintances managed to pry him out of his seclusion and to show him every part of the city. New York didn't please him. He recognized the impressive commerce, the huge size of the buildings, the efficiency of the public services, and all the admirable urban conditions, while at the same time he sensed the city's lack of historical character, those pages of stone in which the European cities testified to centuries past. More than anything else, he felt the lack of that indefinable sense of character that permeated Paris, Rome, Madrid, and Brussels, something that sprang from buildings, people, and language which defined that spirit of a race.

With its blocks of houses arranged geometrically like the squares of a chess board, New York seemed devoid of any personality that might attract a dreamer like himself. The women impressed him as men disguised, and the men seemed to be vacant, walking figures. His prejudices went so far as to cause him to believe that all conversations consisted in relating numbers and statistics, stock market quotations, and bank accounts. Visits seemed to have no other goal than to carry on business or to exchange market prices.

The only thing that relieved his bad mood and homesickness was the hope that at any moment he might receive permission to return to Costa Rica. May passed, then June. Still no word arrived about any amnesty. There was a good reason why the government had not conceded it, and Fernando learned of it from letters secretly sent to him by some friends. If the leaders of the opposition had sold out to the government, the people, nobler and less fickle, continued to protest, however fruitlessly, against the brutal coup d'etat regardless of the repression. Thus, in those circumstances, the presence of the exiled leaders could be the spark igniting a political fire.

At first, Fernando often received letters from Margarita and occasionally some from her parents, but gradually her letters became less frequent as well as briefer. Fernando felt that their tone became cooler, as if they were written more by formula than feeling.

Margarita wrote that some friends — doubtless urged by Don Rafael—came each Sunday to the country house with the intention of cheering her up. They improvised concerts and dances in which she felt obliged to take part. She referred also to Mr. Ward, who was going to offer a huge celebration on the fourth of July, although she didn't think that she'd attend.

Through Doña Virginia, Fernando learned that the Weaving Company, founded by Mr. Ward, had begun to cultivate the Nicoya lands purchased from Don Rafael. In fact, the textile mill there would be in operation within a year.

An incredible anxiety filled the month of August for Fernando. Not one letter arrived from his sweetheart; nor was there one from her parents. Had some misfortune befallen the family? That didn't seem possible because they would have been the first to inform him. Had the government been intercepting their letters? That didn't seem possible either because his fellow exiles received letters from their families and friends. Fernando thought of every possible reason why he hadn't heard from Costa Rica. Eventually he invented an excuse that satisfied him, even filled him with joy: Couldn't it be that Don Rafael's doctor had advised him to travel to the United States for medical reasons and that the family was on its way without telling him so that they could surprise him? That dream delighted Fernando but for a short time!

On September 15, he ran into the former presidential candidate in the hotel lobby. The politician vibrated with excitement. Pulling out a cablegram from the Costa Rican government, he showed Fernando the news: The government announced an amnesty. A few days later as Fernando was packing to leave for home, he received from Doña Virginia a letter whose contents struck him like a bolt of lightening. The letter read,

"My dear Fernando, I've hesitated before writing to you, but the love I feel for you forces me to write now. They say that after September 15, the government will allow you to return home. When you arrive at Puerto Limón, please telegraph me so that I can go to San José to meet you. Then you'll learn the horrible misfortune that has befallen us. It would be much better if you'd never come back! I am old; I am sick; I will not be able to survive this misfortune, but you are young and strong. God will teach you resignation. Pity us!"

IX

Yankee Expansion

To become an instant hero and to hear his name spoken with admiration, any foreigner in San José simply has to dress elegantly, assume a bit of a theatrical air, and—most importantly—spend money freely. The press then devotes plenty of space to him; a crowd of hangers-on surrounds him offering friendship; the oldest and best families fight to have him as their guest; and if the foreigner is relatively young and not too ugly, then there will be at least two or three young ladies vying for his attention. It has happened, and not infrequently, that such a fawned-upon foreigner turned out to be an infamous criminal or ne'er-do-well who when least expected simply disappears from the country after having deflowered one of those gullible local belles. Even repeated examples of this behavior have not been enough to cure the local mania for foreigners. Those people think everything and everyone foreign are superior to everything and everyone national.

From the day he captained the winning soccer team, no one in San José enjoyed more popularity and admiration than Thomas Ward. Everyone soon learned that he was an extremely wealthy bachelor, that he had purchased the best house in the suburb of Otoya and furnished it in oriental luxury, that he was about to open some huge industries, certainly the sources of virtual rivers of gold, and that money already flowed through his fingers like water. That knowledge swayed the opinions of the local aristocracy in his favor. So much so that the handsome gallant never lacked invitations to attend parties and dinners. Uninvited guests flocked to his door. Droves of well-wishers and petitioners hovered about him. Some hoped to find employment in the factories he planned to open; others simply hoped for a handout trusting the generosity of his seemingly endless wealth. Even the Minister of the Treasury—who had discussed loans with him—added to the reputation of the American by praising his intelligence, his grasp of business, and more than anything else, his expeditious way of solving problems.

The fame of Thomas, as the beautiful young ladies of the capital familiarly called him, extended far and wide within the republic. Those who lived in El Higuerón naturally knew all about his attitudes and accomplishments, since friends of Margarita talked about Thomas incessantly, gossiping about him during the Sunday afternoon gatherings at the estate. Don Rafael supposed that the chatter sprang from the fact that the young American also spent Sundays there. They spoke so much about the American that Margarita drew a certain vain satisfaction from knowing that the center of society's attention focused on one of the intimates of the house who often passed entire days there. The news of his frequent presence at El Higuerón had as an immediate consequence an increase in the number of visitors. It became common to organize weekly dances or concerts at which the hero displayed new and surprising talents. He not only danced expertly the latest steps from the United States, so much in vogue in all the Latin American nations, even those that most vehemently protested Yankee influence, but in addition he possessed a well-trained baritone voice.

With Señorita Montalvo, Thomas was courteous and attentive without ever being aggressive or impertinent. Quick to satisfy her slightest desires, he always behaved so discretely that the capricious young lady could not refuse to accept his kind gestures. In that way, heady from the intoxicating atmosphere of admiration that surrounded the young gentleman, she came to feel a sincere tenderness for him.

In order to celebrate appropriately the fourth of July, the anniversary of his nation's independence, Mr. Ward decided to offer a grand ball in his home, which also served as the consulate, since it was impossible to hold it in the legation because of the recent period of mourning of the death of the minister.

If Fernando had witnessd the preparations for that ball on the part of the republic's elite, he would have been convinced of the uselessness of his campaign against ostentatious luxury and of the hypocricy of the praise given his moralizing dramas. The shops in the capital bustled with activity. The owners and clerks brought out the finest textiles, shoes, gloves, hats, belts, and adornments to meet the excessive demands of anxious young ladies eager to accentuate their beauty or at least to minimize their homeliness.

What hardships, sacrifices, and difficulties were caused by the preparations for such a glorious evening! There were even those who spent a whole month's salary for the proper attire. One father even mortgaged the family home in order to properly dress his daughters for the occasion. The party gave every promise of being the grandest ever held in the capital. All the government and diplomatic officials would attend since Mr. Ward was the consul of the United States.

His residence, the largest and most elegant of Otoya, was situated in the middle of a large yard carpeted with grass. Flowers surrounded the house as did myriad plants none so tall that it would prevent anyone from the street from appreciating fully the architectural beauty of the house and its setting. In the back a curtain of trees further set off the house. Small paths meandered among the trees. Benches and a gazebo added to the attractiveness.

On the night of July fourth, pedestrians stopped dazzled in their tracks before the opulent mansion. It glittered like a precious stone in the sunlight. Above the granite portico a thousand small electric lights formed the patterns of the Costa Rican and United States flags. Chinese lanterns of many shapes illuminated the walk from the gate to the house. Lanterns hanging in the trees behind the house created a fairyland scene.

On the ground floor of the house the rooms were arranged with supreme elegance. The principal room, the ample ballroom with its small game rooms, displayed collections of art and Indian antiquities with that order, discrimination, and magnificence that reveal a combination of good taste with a sizeable bank account.

Mr. Ward had personally invited Don Rafael and his family, but the old man and his sister had influenza and couldn't attend. Furthermore, they were not fond of formal dances, which, in their opinion, had been invented more to display wealth and beautiful gowns than as an amusement. The foreigner insisted that Margarita be allowed to attend. Señor Montalvo agreed to permit his daughter to go to the ball, accompanied by the Valdés sisters, the same young ladies who had been with her at the theater the night Fernando's play had premiered. At first, Margarita politely but unconvincingly refused to attend, but at her age it isn't easy to resist temptations of that kind, particularly when she felt a secret desire to see herself courted in public by the very man whom all the young ladies of the capital had tried to capture with their winning looks.

When Margarita entered the ballroom on the arm of the American, she was greeted by a murmur of universal admiration. She looked beautiful in her white dress, perfectly tailored and superbly adorned. She wore no jewels except a diamond hairclip that crowned her elegant coiffure. Her beauty, highlighted by simplicity of dress, attracted the attention of everyone. When the orchestra began the first waltz after they had played the national anthems of both nations, the quiet whispers became audible praise for the couple. Everyone said that they had never seen such a graceful couple nor one that could dance better.

Mr. Ward seemed oblivious to all these remarks and attention. Not so for Margarita. She felt herself envied by the women and admired by the men whose praise she could overhear. When she returned to her seat compliments rained down on her. One elderly spinster at her side exclaimed, "Heavens, what a perfect couple. You were made for each other. I could spend the rest of the evening watching the two of you dance."

Blushing, Margarita lowered her eyes, while the Yankee asked permission to reserve the best numbers on her dance card. They danced together a number of times before dinner. Each time they won anew the admiration of the others who pulled back to give them sufficient room on the floor to dance. Margarita felt an unusual rapture as she glided across the floor with her eyes half closed, her heart beating feverishly, as she felt the pressure of that strong arm that seemed to guide her through space. The words of the foreigner caressed her ears and further weakened her. She felt her will power slowly crumble beneath the weight of his sweetly imperative voice. In the powder room, her friends gushed their congratulations, although most of them lacked sincerity. Luisa Valdés made a few jokes about her new conquest without paying much attention to Margarita's protests. According to Luisa, preference of the American for Margarita was so obvious that Alicia Martínez, a ravishingly beautiful blonde who, according to the gossip, was crazy about Mr. Ward, had left the party on the pretext of a sudden headache.

In the dining room, there was a separate table for the host, the Minister of Finance, Margarita, and the Valdés family. During the dinner, the Minister commented discretely on the major news event, the North American protectorate of Nicaragua, which the press reported had recently been established.

"In Latin America," said Mr. Ward, "it is believed that my country avidly seeks new conquests. Nothing could be farther from the truth. We want the best relations with these republics, but we can't remain indifferent when they destroy themselves with civil wars caused by ambition or greed and when there are no guarantees either for nationals or foreigners."

"What you're saying," interjected Luisa Valdés, "is that if the Costa Ricans begin to fight among themselves the same thing will happen to us as happened to Nicaraguans."

"As the interim counsel, I can't say anything," Mr. Ward replied with a smile. "But if it were up to me I would advocate annexation rather than a protectorate for Costa Rica."

"You!"

"Yes, so that I could become a Costa Rican without giving up my American citizenship."

Luisa cast a meaningful glance at Margarita and then standing up suggested, "While the others are finishing dinner why don't we take a stroll in the garden? It looks so attractive."

The others accepted her suggestion, and the lively young lady led them outdoors where she was joined by her fiancée, who had followed to be with her.

Besides the large blue lanterns located at intervals among the trees, hundreds of small bulbs of the same color, hidden among the foliage like lightening bugs, shed an ethereal light. The scene might have been from a fairy tale, so removed was it from worldly realities. The Yankee and Margarita sat together on a garden bench and conversed in the confidential tones of two people who after their initial indifference toward each other were now drawn together by mutual and strong ties of affection. Doubtless the excitement of the ball, the beauty of their surroundings, and above all else the admiration of the crowd had helped to close the distance that had once separated those two. Without affectation, he spoke of his travels, his ambitions, and his life. He had no other relatives alive except two married brothers, one in San Francicso and the other in Canada. She listened as if enchanted by his stories. As she reflected on his life, which seemed a rare combination of happiness and solitary melancholy, a feeling of tenderness toward him overwhelmed her.

"A life without love is very sad," said Mr. Ward. "But it is infinitely sadder to see happiness in front of you without being able to grasp it, to live without being able to touch the one you love, to die without anyone shedding a tear for you."

"Oh, don't say such things," Margarita sighed without being able to contain herself any longer.

"Listen, Margarita," he went on with a gentle yet vibrantly emotional voice, "I never knew what love was until I came to Costa Rica. The love I now feel is so impossible, so much without any hope that I've decided to go away, very far, perhaps to some place with an unhealthy climate with the hope of ending this miserable life as quickly as possible. Should I go away? Tell me."

From the ballroom those sounds of romantic music filled the night air. The American gazed steadily at his companion and the hand he had resting on the back of the bench moved until it touched hers which he took hold of without meeting any resistance.

"Go away? Why?" she murmured lowering her head.

"And *you* . . . *you* would ask me why!"

Margarita quickly withdrew her hand. Luisa Valdés on the arm of her boyfriend and followed by other couples was approaching. She exclaimed, "My friends, the orchestra is playing. Oh, Mr. Ward, this garden is enchanting, bewitching, a paradise."

The party ended at three in the morning. Mr. Ward drove the Valdés family and Margarita home. She sat next to him. They seldom spoke as the car moved through the quiet streets. When he turned his eyes on the beautiful face of his companion, they caught from time to time in the semi-darkness of the car her eyes which under his gaze became timid. At the same time, he felt her warm and loveable body pressed closely against his.

When she awoke the following day, Margarita's eyes were red and swollen as if she had cried the entire night.

X

Under
The Tree

No matter how much Doña Virginia thought about it, exercising all the wits that God gave her, she couldn't fathom the change that took place in her niece after the party at the American consulate. Very melancholic, even unsociable, after Fernando first went into exile, Margarita now played the piano more frequently, took excursions around the estate on foot or horseback, and enjoyed the visitors who previously had bored her. The strangest part was that after a period of exhilaration she would suddenly become sad like someone who had enjoyed herself in order to forget something and then felt even more sharply pangs of remorse. Another symptom alarming to the older lady was that her young niece no longer spent hour after hour talking with her about the absent lover, nor did she seem as upset as she once was when the mails were delayed. Had some change come over her or was it simply that the prolonged separation had dampened old feelings?

Understanding her niece better than anyone, she knew it was useless to force her to explain what it was all about before she was willing to do so spontaneously. The most prudent way was to observe her when she was with others or to worm some information out of her friends who spent Sundays with them on the estate.

Unfortunately before she could carry out her plan, a serious case of bronchitis confined her to bed. The weather turned unpleasant and humid. The clouds stirred by the wind enveloped the house, showered a fine, cold rain on the pastures forcing the livestock to voluntarily seek refuge in the barns and the workers to shiver from the cold.

Mr. Ward didn't show up at El Higuerón until five days after the ball. His absence annoyed Don Rafael because the American had promised him he would oversee the installation of the electrical plant to provide lighting as well as other needs for the estate. A nearby waterfall was to furnish the power for the plant.

Finally he arrived on horseback bundled up in his rain gear. The principal reason for his visit he informed them was to see how Doña Virginia was, since he had heard of her illness through one of their servants who had gone to the capital for medicine. He also wanted to resolve some difficulties he'd encountered with governmental bureaucracy about registering those lands he'd purchased from Señor Montalvo. He had brought with him the plans for the electrical plant, news that Don Rafael received with unrestrained joy.

"Ah, now," said the old man, "you're not going to leave me until we've begun work on that plant. No excuses! It may be boring to you to spend a few days here at work but count it as a sacrifice for your friends."

At that moment Margarita arrived. If her father had not been so absorbed with the plans the Yankee had brought him, he would have noticed the unusual tension in which the two young people greeted each other. They sat in the living room, and after some brief conversation Don Rafael told Margarita, "Call the servant to prepare a room for Mr. Ward. He's going to spend a few days with us."

"Please don't bother," the American said to the young woman who looked at him with surprise. "I have a lot to do in San José. In fact, I must return today."

"In this weather! Impossible! At least stay with us until tomorrow, even if it bores you."

"Bores me! In this hospitable home! How can you say such a thing, Don Rafael? But. . . ."

"Ah, good, then, no excuse. You'll stay."

Mr. Ward glanced again at Margarita who without saying a word left the room to speak to the servant.

At midday, the American spent almost an hour with Doña Virginia, trying to amuse her with jokes and conversation and then he prepared for her a kind of hot grog with whiskey, a drink that in his country was considered an infallible remedy for any type of cold and thus good for her respiratory ailment.

Since the weather had cleared by late afternoon, the two men strolled in the garden and chatted. Once again the topic of the North American protectorate of Nicaragua surfaced in their conversation. Don Rafael had been reading a good deal about it in all the newspapers. It is easy to imagine the bitter criticism the old man leveled at the Great Republic for intervening. It offended his patriotism—or his chauvinism as Mr. Ward termed it. He disliked it because the intervention threatened both the integrity and the good name of all Spanish-speaking nations.

That evening after the dinner celebrating the Americans' soccer victory, Don Rafael had promised Fernando that one day he would confront Mr. Ward with his accusations. Their leisure hours during his visit provided just the occasion, but much to Don Rafael's surprise, the Yankee disapproved of the imperialist policies of his own government.

"My official duties, which happily won't last much longer," he replied with a smile, "don't allow me to make public my opinions. However, among friends, I tell you that my country committed a serious error by imposing its will by force on these republics. It offends them deeply, and furthermore, it creates a feeling of lack of confidence in the other American nations. How much better it would be to aid them in improving their moral, economic, and political conditions! They would appreciate us then and not hate us."

"The best thing," replied Don Rafael, "is to leave us alone to remedy our own ills. We know our problems better than anyone else."

"But haven't you already enjoyed a century of independence—just a few years less than we have—without being able to remedy your own ills? From our country we sadly watch endless chaos, frequent violations of law, and countless civil wars."

"One thing is the ambitious politicians," Don Rafael went on, "that fatal plague of Central America, and another is the innocent and hard working people who are exploited and corrupted."

"Yes, but if the educated citizens, to whom I refer as the real people, shake off their selfishness and apathy to demand a strict accounting from the transgressors I'm sure they'll end their abuse because even a weak person gets respect when he shows his determination. Don't fool yourself, Don Rafael, most of the former Spanish colonies were not prepared for republican governments when they declared their independence nor have they bothered since then to educate themselves in any practical way to enjoy liberty or to exercise their rights. For three years I've been studying these people as I am accustomed to do wherever I live, and I've read nearly all the books and essays about them. Frankly, if I were a Costa Rican, there are many pages I'd tear out of *The Official Gazette*. For example, there was a period when presidents entered and left office as if the presidential palace had a revolving door. Each new chief of state brought with him a group of cronies. The city governments wasted their new funds on banquets for the new leaders, while school children spent their time learning poems to recite to them on official occasions."

"Don't you understand that the authorities required them to do that? Anyway, it doesn't happen like that any more."

"Perhaps not, but the picture today is really no prettier. The people give themselves over uninhibitedly to drink. The farmers slowly abandon their work habits and look for jobs as policemen or soldiers. The republic has become a vast bureaucracy. Right now it's ready to go down the drain. You'll see," added Mr. Ward as Don Rafael made a gesture of protest. "A doctor friend of mine from the United States who is here to combat the hookworm so prevalent in this country, asked the government in a report published in the official governmental newspaper to enact a law to require the people to seek a cure for the disease because hundreds of those inflicted by it just ignore it."

"Good heavens," exclaimed a by now exasperated Señor Montalvo, "what right do foreigners have to meddle in our affairs trying to correct our defects?"

"Our duty to our fellow man guides us. I don't want my country to absorb the Latins, and I don't believe it intends to, but the day it wants to do so it won't encounter any insurmountable obstacle because the Latins themselves have smoothed the way. Haven't you people already adopted with enthusiasm the dress, customs, dances, and even the games of the United States? The young men go there to finish their studies; the young ladies imitate in every detail the ways of the women of my country. Your newspapers publish at least one page in English and the school children give more care to learning English than they do to their own language. We're not the ones who want to turn you into Yankees; you yourselves are eager to give up being Costa Ricans."

The discussion was becoming increasingly heated when Margarita arrived opportunely to defuse it. She reminded her father that the farm workers had arrived to receive their weekly salary. The old man left with his head bowed, nearly in tears, while the two young people remained alone.

Margarita stood there, somewhat uncertain, her eyes fixed on the ground. She made no movement to leave. Mr. Ward spoke sweetly to her, "Don't you want to sit down?" She obeyed without looking at him and for the moment only the songs of the birds broke the silence. They filled the branches of the fig tree at sundown. Then the American approached her and bent down so that she was obliged to raise her eyes. He whispered, "Margarita, that night at the party was the happiest of my life. I told you I was thinking of going away and you asked me why. Now, that you know the reason why I might leave, I want to ask you if I should go."

She lowered her eyes again and blushed. Her beautiful chest beat violently under her blue silk blouse.

"Should I go?" he repeated insistently.

"No," she whispered in a barely audible voice.

"Margarita," he exclaimed happily, "think what that one small word means for you . . . for me. Say it again! Should I go?"

"No," she repeated covering her face with her hands. He gently took hold of them and moved still closer to her, but Margarita stood up and looking at him with pleading eyes said, "Let's go in now. It's already dark."

Mr. Ward remained only a few days at El Higuerón, but they were sufficient for him to get the work on the electrical plant well underway much to the delight of the proprietor. The bad weather continued. It rained torrents, especially in the afternoons. Not one afternoon afforded Don Rafael the pleasure of sunning himself beneath his favorite tree. Either because of the weather or old age or a bit of both, he began to complain of rheumatic pains in his right arm and leg. For that reason and also because Doña Virginia continued to suffer from bronchitis, the doctor advised the family to leave for San José, where the weather was less rigorous and where they would be closer to all forms of medical attention.

At first, Don Rafael resisted. Only when Mr. Ward promised to go each morning to supervise the work on the electrical plant and because Fermín was perfectly capable of taking care of the milk production did Señor Montalvo resign himself to the necessity of following the doctor's suggestion. One morning he loaded the family in a huge wagon, the only vehicle capable of conquering the mire created by the storms, and six hours later they arrived somewhat shaken by the rough journey at their spacious house in the capital.

The change benefitted the two sick ones, even if one, accustomed to the active life of the farm, felt bored within four walls and the other missed her flowers, chickens, and aviary. As for Margarita, her character had been transformed: She seemed calm and reserved without any trace of the extremes of joy and depression that had so worried Doña Virginia. She frequently went out alone or accompanied by her friends, and she seemed to have acquired a distinct aversion to reading. Furthermore, she never wrote. To an observation of Doña Virginia that Fernando seemed to have been forgotten, she dryly replied, "How can I answer letters I never receive?" Not one but three letters had arrived recently for her, but the strange young woman had hidden them without saying a word to anyone.

From the first, the suspicions of the aunt focused on the American. For Margarita to change in such a manner it was necessary for a new love to have eclipsed the old one in her heart. No young man except Mr. Ward visited the house; none lingered in the street in front of the house. The Yankee came often but he spent most of his time talking with Don Rafael without addressing more than a few words to Margarita. Doña Virginia redoubled her vigilence but still could not discover any evidence in support of her suspicions. Two or three times it seemed to her that Mr.

Ward and her niece exchanged meaningful glances, and on one occasion she thought she saw them furtively exchange a note as they were saying goodbye. Still, the serenity of the young woman was so complete, and the indifference with which she received the foreigner so noticeable, that the suspicious aunt finally convinced herself that the problem was that no letters arrived from New York.

XI

A Shadow Falls

As THE DAYS PASSED, Don Rafael's regard for Thomas Ward increased, a regard that very soon became sincere admiration and gratitude. That intelligent and energetic young man who knew everything and attempted everything, who undertook risky ventures more as a challenge than as an effort to augment his already sizeable income, had become indispensible in the Montalvo household. Thanks to his efforts the output of the hacienda had nearly tripled: The hygienic barn constructed under his guidance had cut down livestock diseases, the workers seemed more dedicated, and even the overseer Fermín obeyed his orders more quickly.

What was even more astonishing was that Mr. Ward seemed to find plenty of time to do everything. Without neglecting the installation of the electrical plant nor the other improvements he'd offered to make on the farm, he attended to his own affairs and even went twice to Nicoya to oversee the preparation and planting of the lands he'd bought from Señor Montalvo.

The entire family found itself under the foreigner's

powerful spell. Even Doña Virginia, who at first hadn't really liked him, capitulated finally to his friendliness and courtesy, a capitulation facilitated by the memories of the solicitous attention she'd received from him during her illness. Their affection for him did not mean that Don Rafael and his sister had forgotten Fernando. They often spoke fondly of him and learned with joy the news that the government was thinking of decreeing on September 15, a general amnesty for all political exiles. To tell the truth, though, Don Rafael never had put much faith in the formal betrothal of his daughter to Fernando Rodríguez, partly because he knew the fickle nature of his daughter and partly because the caution and outward frigidity of the young lawyer seemed to place his feelings somewhere between friendship and true love. He had not been displeased with the thought of the marriage, to which he readily consented as a formality, but deep inside he had not felt any strong urge to support Fernando's candidacy for his daughter's hand if a competitor appeared, particularly one who could handle his business affairs astutely. For those reasons, although he recognized the changes in Margarita, he didn't ascribe much importance to them nor did he pay much attention to Doña Virginia's observations on the matter.

He did become upset near the end of August when his sister noted that the young girl's health was less than robust. She lost her appetite, grew paler, and seemed sadder, isolating herself in her room. The only person she seemed to enjoy seeing was Luisa Valdés, her closest friend, who stopped by nearly every afternoon to pick up Margarita and take her to her house in the Otoya district. Luisa belonged to one of the most distinguished families in the capital. Totally pampered, she had been brought up rather permissively. She was neither as pretty nor as wise as her sister Emilia, but she supplemented her deficiencies with a liveliness, and easy-going nature, and wit that attracted numerous followers but at the same time caused tongues in the capital to wag—and the gossip was not always kind to the young lady.

If Don Rafael and his prudent sister had heard only half the stories they would have put an immediate end to the daily visits Margarita paid to the house of her friend. However, since both held the Valdés family in highest esteem and because Margarita always was home before ten in the evening accompanied by Luisa and her brother, a sixteen-year-old student, they saw no reason to prohibit her single entertainment.

Mr. Ward never stopped by in the evening. He limited his visits to mid-day following his visit to El Higuerón, and the reason for those visits was to inform Don Rafael of the progress of the various projects. Occasionally he stayed for lunch, but usually he excused himself because he had other work to attend to.

Whether by chance or because of the language or manner of Margarita, her friends began to stop visiting the house, much to the amazement of Doña Virginia. She couldn't understand what was happening, nor why, and the more she thought about it the less able she was to come up with a satisfactory answer. It puzzled and frustrated her. That her niece no longer loved Fernando, if indeed she had ever loved anyone, couldn't be more obvious. And, if that was true, who had caught her attention? Her thoughts, after they had entertained every possibility, even the remotest, stubbornly returned to her original suspicion, to that foreigner who seemed to have hypnotized everyone. But she was confused. Nothing existed to indicate that there was anything of interest between her niece and Mr. Ward. She finally arrived at the conclusion that the key to the mystery lay in the evening visits to the house of Luisa Valdés.

Quickly, the old woman devised a plan. The next night she would go under some pretext to pick up Margarita and that way she'd find out if the two girls were alone or accompanied by some admirers. She resolved, furthermore, to spy on the return home of her niece to see whether or not it was only Luisa and her little brother who

Amighetti
Costa Rica 931—

accompanied her or whether in fact someone older and less innocent than the student also was with her niece. Doña Virginia devised another plan to attempt to measure the degree of feelings that might exist between Margarita and Mr. Ward. To end all doubts, she decided to find an opportunity to leave the two alone in a room while she watched them secretly from another. She would then learn whether the indifference with which they treated each other in public was a refined hypocrisy. Their behavior alone could remove all the doubts that old woman harbored.

It was necessary, however, to postpone the second part of her plan because the American suddenly left for his plantation at Nicoya and would not return until the weekend. Neither was she able to implement the first part because for several nights Luisa practiced her piano and guitar lessons at Margarita's. She said that she couldn't do it at home because the music disturbed a neighbor who was sick.

On those very nights an unusual event occurred that increased the perplexity of uneasiness of Doña Virginia. The bedroom of her niece was separated from hers by a wall of reinforced concrete. Nonetheless, one night she heard smothered sobs that could come from no other place than the girl's bedroom. Alarmed, she knocked on the wall several times, asking, "What's the matter, Margarita?"

Receiving no answer, she assumed that her niece had had a nightmare. After the sobs were heard a couple of nights later, Doña Virginia questioned Margarita the following morning. Her red eyes provided the answer.

"It's nothing, Mother," she answered with difficulty. "You know my nervous temperament. I've always been that way."

"Why don't you tell me your problem?"

"I said there was nothing wrong," Margarita insisted a bit testily. She ran to her room and closed the door. Her aunt's eyes followed her. The old woman was surprised.

She'd never heard her niece speak to her before in that tone of voice.

On his first visit after his return to the capital, Mr. Ward announced to the family that he would leave for California to buy the machinery for Le Ceiba and to see his older brother, who was one of the principal stockholders of the Weaving Company. That occasion favored the plan of Doña Virginia who observed attentively but subtly the effect of that news on Margarita. Her careful planning produced no result. Margarita accepted the news with total indifference. His departure was set for September 5. Mr. Ward would take the midnight express train for Puntarenas, from where his ship would leave at dawn.

At noon on the day before his departure, he called on the family to say goodby. He arrived just as Don Rafael was preparing to go by horse to the farm. Word had just reached him that a bull had seriously wounded Fermín with his horns. The American's visit was extremely short. He excused himself for not being able to return the following day because he had still not finished the preparations for his trip. Don Rafael spent that night at El Higuerón, and the following morning sent a note to tell his family that he probably won't return to the capital that day because the overseer continued to be in serious condition and the torrential rains made travel on the road hazardous.

Very early on September 5, Luisa Valdés called at the house to ask her friend to go shopping with her. Later Margarita retired to her room, and Doña Virginia, who was reading in her own, could hear her opening and closing drawers. The young girl ate hardly any lunch and spent the afternoon leafing through books and magazines in the living room. At eight she went to bed complaining of a severe headache. Her aunt retired early also after checking to make sure that all the doors were securely locked. Some vague apprehension, however, made her restless. She tossed and turned without being able to sleep, although she heard no sound from either Margarita's room or from anywhere else in the house.

Around eleven a car horn sounded in the street and
the auto sped by. Soon thereafter the muffled sound of a
car motor could be heard. It seemed to be parked only a
short distance from the house. Almost at once, Doña
Virginia heard the slight squeaking of floorboards in the
next room as if someone were moving around very carefully. She strained to hear, hardly breathing as she listened. She could hear the latch of a door moving ever so slowly and silently.

At that momemt, a horrible thought overcame her.
Without putting on her robe or turning on the light she
went to the door of her room and carefully opened it a
crack so that she could see down the hallway weakly illuminated by a small electric light. She surveyed the hall
for only a few seconds when a figure stealthily emerged
from the next room. Before she could even let out a scream
of terror, she saw a woman wrapped in a fur coat, her face
covered with a heavy veil, slip down the hallway. At that
point, Doña Virginia threw open the door and demanded,
"Where are you going, Margarita?"

The young woman quickly turned, dropping the small
suitcase she carried, and let out a scream that reverberated
throughout the house.

"What is this? Where are you headed?" Doña Virginia
repeated. Seeing that she wavered as if she were about to
collapse, the woman rushed forward with arms extended.
Margarita fell into them sobbing and screaming at the same
time in hysteria. Doña Virginia helped her to her bed and
tried to calm her.

Emotionally disturbed, Margarita struggled to free
herself shouting, "I want to kill myself! Everything is lost!
I've no hope! I've been awful! Let me alone. I don't want
anyone to see me again, ever." With a strength unusual for
her age, Doña Virginia managed to hold her down on the
bed while she tried to calm her with reason and affection.
Finally the crisis passed, and Margarita, bathed in tears,
rested her head in her aunt's lap.

In that modest, dimly lighted room and in the silence of the night, the old woman listened with tears streaming down her own cheeks to the complete confession of what had happened, the whole dismal drama. It was a classic tale of seduction. It began the night of the dance and continued without letup at El Higuerón. The foreigner, who enjoyed such an enviable reputation in Costa Rica, had suggested and pressed the temptation. Luisa Valdés also played an ignoble role, one that hastened the predicament of Margarita. Together they made secret visits to the Yankee's home where Luisa also met her lover. The nocturnal flight was an attempt to avoid public scandal. She hoped to hide her dishonor in a foreign land among unknown people.

As Doña Virginia listened in silence, her heart sank, paralyzed by pain. The confession crushed her. It was as if the universe had fallen on her. The tears flowed and soaked the hair of the unhappy young woman whose head rested in her lap. So distraught was she that it didn't occur to her to make an effort to stop the fugitive and seducer, who at that moment was leaving the country.

About an hour before dawn, the emotional crisis of Margarita recurred with such intensity and violence that Doña Virginia had to use morphine to calm her. Fortunately the servants lived in another wing of the house, far from the noise of the drama. They heard nothing of the extraordinary events that unfolded that night, and therefore they had no tales to tell the following day. About six in the morning, Doña Virginia wrote and dispatched a brief note to her brother at El Higuerón. She then shut herself in the room with Margarita, fell to her knees near the head of the drowsing girl and began to pray.

XII

The Return

IMPATIENTLY FERNANDO awaited the departure of the ship that would return him to his homeland. Hurricanes pounding the east coast of the United States had delayed the ship's departure for two days. The enigmatic letter from Doña Virginia had so disturbed him that he felt that if the ship didn't leave soon he was capable of attempting the journey in a rowboat just to get on the way and to end his uncertainty.

What awaited him in Costa Rica? What would he learn? His mind jumped between two equally unpleasant thoughts of which one—the death of Margarita—seemed more and more real, the only possible explanation of past mysteries. The other thought, that she might no longer love him, seemed absurd, too far fetched to be believed. Finally the weather improved enough for the ship to hoist anchor. Fernando and his three traveling companions bid farewell to that country which was so different from their own and seemed so cold toward them and, yet, at the same time, had offered them a hospitality and freedom their own country had denied them.

The early October sea was choppy and turbulent along the North American coast, but once they reached the Caribbean the ship sailed through the calmest of waters with daily afternoon showers. The trip seemed far too long and exceedingly slow to Fernando. Seated in a deck chair, he passed endless hours contemplating the sea. Sometimes its rhythmic movement brought back memories of that night (it seemed so long ago now) when he had looked out over a sea of faces in the National Theater and heard the waves of applause from thousands of clapping hands greeting the premiere of his play.

More often than not, his thoughts concentrated on his present situation and the conditions of his country. How would he spend his time now? To what would he devote his energies? Could he continue his campaign to reawaken the national consciousness? Would he be permitted to write about the national vices as he saw them, to offer his plays on themes of public morality? The outcome of the political tragicomedy in which he had been both actor and spectator had cooled his patriotic ardor and dimmed his hopes. He had witnessed the leaders of the opposition party humbly bow before the new political idol imposed and supported by bayonets. He knew that the people had accepted their new master and that even the most rebellious members of the opposition had been silenced with bribes and favors. But he also understood that not withstanding all of this there still were honest, courageous, and conscientious Costa Ricans who knew their duty, but how, he wondered, could this small and impotent group begin again the campaign to regenerate the nation.

"We're lost, hopelessly lost!" Fernando sighed bitterly. Without wanting to, he recalled the somber picture drawn by Mr. Ward: A sick people who refused to cure themselves, who even refused to speak of their illness. He also recalled that other diseased entity, the handsome, statly fig tree that at first glance looked so healthy, whose owner refused to recognize, even to see, the deadly rot.

When he disembarked in Puerto Limón, Fernando had made up his mind. He would marry Margarita, sell all his properties, and move to Europe. He would not return to Costa Rica until his country reformed, became worthy of the name of a republic, and extended to all citizens the equal protection of the law.

As Doña Virginia had instructed, Fernando sent her a telegram announcing his arrival and then boarded the next train for the capital where he arrived at nine o'clock that night. The exiles found three or four friends waiting. They had hurried to the station defying the ire of the government. Also present were some party members from the working class. The police were on hand to observe the proceedings.

Fernando immediately asked one of his acquaintances for news about the Montalvo family. Instead of the tragic news he had expected, he heard with surprise that except for Don Rafael's sickness and some slight illness of his sister nothing unusual had happened at El Higuerón.

In passing, his friends mentioned a scandal that had stunned society. Luisa Valdés had run away with her boyfriend. The two fled the country on the same ship Mr. Ward took. Had the American played a role in their escape? Or was his presence just a coincidence?

Fernando could not sleep that night, less because of the excitement of returning to San José than because he anxiously awaited dawn so that he could lay to rest once and for all the uncertainties that perplexed him. He arose early and from eight o'clock onward he watched the door expecting a message from Doña Virginia. He was just about to go to the Montalvo house when Fermín arrived on horseback to tell him that the old woman was waiting for him.

Obviously the messenger was glad to see the lawyer back. He liked him, and he grasped his hand in that delightfully familiar way that characterized Costa Rican peasants. To the questions Fernando asked, he replied sadly and with a sigh, "Oh señor, they've been there for a month, and since they've returned to the farm the young lady Margarita is real sad and nothing can make her come out of her room. Poor old Don Rafael is in a bad way. He had a heart attack. Can't move his right leg. Can't move the right arm neither."

Without losing another second, Fernando took off for the suburb of Amon, while Fermin went in the opposite direction to the market in order to buy some goods.

Although all the windows of the house were tightly closed, the main door stood ajar. Fernando entered after pressing the electric door button. He stopped at the living room door. In one corner of the room, he spotted Doña Virginia, bent over, her elbows on her knees, holding a handkerchief to her eyes. The young man rushed to her to greet her affectionately. She embraced him without being able to say a word between her bitter sobs.

"But, what is it, what happened for God's sake?" the distraught Fernando shouted. "What is everyone hiding from me? Speak! Tell me everything. Has Margarita died? I want the truth."

"It might have been better had she died," murmured Doña Virginia, her voice broken by her sobs.

Fernando froze, petrified. He felt as if someone had poured a bucket of ice water over him. He stared stupified at the old woman. His intuition told him at once what had happened. He covered his face with his hands and fell into a chair.

Now it was Doña Virginia's turn to comfort him. Putting a hand on his shoulder, she said sadly, "My poor friend, I wish you hadn't returned. You must know the truth, and I have to be the one to tell you. Rafael and I cannot endure this heavy blow. We'll never be the same, but you . . . you're young . . . in time you'll forget . . . and forgive her."

Her throat was tight with pain as she sat next to Fernando who remained motionless, immobilized by sadness.

Slowly the old woman began to tell the tragic story. She hid nothing: the insidious behavior of the foreigner, the infamous acts of Luisa, the terrible revelations of Margarita, and finally the dramatic scene when Don Rafael arrived the day after the frustrated flight.

"My poor brother! You can't possibly imagine his desperation. He wanted to kill her and then commit suicide! You can't imagine how difficult it was for me to prevent these new misfortunes and to convince him that we should leave at once for the farm. I went by coach with our disgraced daughter. He went at night alone. The next day he suffered a heart attack that paralyzed him. He won't pardon her, and he doesn't ever want to see her again. The distraught girl never leaves her room. Ay! Why has God forgotten us?"

Pale, eyes downcast, Fernando listened. After she finished the story, Fernando muttered, "The real culprit has escaped!"

"Yes, and he'll never return. Haven't you read the announcement he put in the newspapers? He plans to live in New York and his brother who lives in California will come here to run the business."

Fernando stood up. He spoke resolutely, "Doña Virginia, I'll accompany you to the farm. I need to talk to Don Rafael today."

"Speak to him? Impossible! He . . . can't . . . he doesn't want to. He'll die of shame. You should have seen how he cried last night when I showed him your telegram."

"If you don't want me to accompany you, I'll go alone," Fernando insisted.

Understanding the firm determination of the young man, Doña Virginia gave in. A half-hour later they were on their way to the country followed by Fermín, who didn't stop repeating, "Now you'll see. The boss will be pleased to see you. Everyone's gonna be happy when you arrive, Don Fernando!"

How monotonous and sad the trip now seemed to Fernando when he had previously raced along the road, his heart filled with love and dreams. The sounds of the horses echoed emptily. Sadness gripped his soul. All had changed. A journey once of joy became a funeral march. Doña Virginia also sat in silence, lost in thought. She spoke only to order Fermín to ride ahead to prepare Don Rafael for their arrival.

Fermín found his master seated in the sun on his favorite bench. The poor old man did not want to see Fernando. He ordered his servants to carry him to his room. The interview was painful. The two men embraced each other for a long time. The old man's desperation was so total that Fernando felt tears in his eyes for the first time. When he was able to overcome some of the emotion, he said in a solemn voice, "Don Rafael, there is still time to prevent a public scandal and to save everyone's honor. I'll take charge of that, and I'll succeed. I swear it."

Señor Montalvo slowly shook his head as he whispered, "To disgrace me! To dishonor an old man! Ay! Why didn't God give me a son?

"Lacking a son," Fernando replied, "You have a friend who knows his duty and will do it."

Later, taking Doña Virginia aside, he said softly, "Before I go, I'd like to speak with her."

"With *her*? Impossible! It would be too cruel on your part."

"If that's the case, then do me the favor of telling her what I've just said to Don Rafael. Tell her I pardon any pain she has caused me and far from being angry because she has ruined my life, I'll see to it that very soon she can face the world again without shame and live happily at the side of the man she loves."

"What are you planning to do? Where are you going?" asked Doña Virginia, disturbed to see that the young man was preparing to leave.

"I'm going away," Fernando answered. He left the house without looking back, as though he might fear regretting the decision he had made.

XIII

Face to Face

As soon as he had finished eating, Thomas Ward went to his study to check his mail. Lounging on a couch of Russian leather beside his handsome mahogany desk, he radiated the satisfaction not only of just having finished an exquisite gourmet meal but also of knowing that his businesses were going exceptionally well, providing him impressive daily profits.

He lit a Havana cigar and began to rummage through the letters. Some he simply tossed into a nearby wastebasket, others he carefully stacked on his desk. Although his study was in the interior of the building, the deafening and continuous noises of automobiles, buses, and vehicles of every description could still be heard. After all, Fourteenth Street was one of the busiest—and thus noisiest—in New York.

Suddenly the Yankee pulled from the pile of letters one whose envelope he examined attentively, as if he recognized the handwriting. The stationery bore the letterhead of the Hotel Astoria and contained only four lines, which Mr. Ward read and reread without being able to hide his surprise. Then he folded the paper and stuck it in his pocket and, glancing at the bronze clock on the mantle, murmured to himself, "Eight o'clock already!" He sat half meditating, half listening to the street noises. Barely ten minutes had passed when he detected sounds of a car at the front curb and then the doorbell. Shortly thereafter the maid entered carrying a calling card and asked, "Shall I show the gentleman waiting in the hall into the living room?"

"No," Mr. Ward decided. "Bring him in here and make sure that no one interrupts us." Then, getting up from the couch, he seated himself at his desk. He opened the top drawer far enough to reveal a shiny metal object and waited with his eyes fixed on the door where a proud Fernando Rodríguez had just appeared.

The lawyer wore a black suit and his expression was not meant to instill tranquility. The American stood up and said courteously, "Please come in and sit down. I've just finished reading your note. If I'd received it earlier I would have come to meet you at your hotel."

Without accepting the polite invitation and even without returning the greeting, Fernando remained standing on the threshhold. He glared at Mr. Ward and spoke dryly, "I arrived in New York only a few hours ago, and tomorrow I leave again for my country. I don't have any time to lose. You doubtless know why I am here."

"To judge from your note, you probably are here to discuss an intimate matter that concerns only me and one other person. Is that it?"

"You're wrong. Toward that other person I have three duties as a gentleman, Costa Rican, and friend. In that capacity, I am here to see that you correct the wrong you have inflicted. Either you marry the young lady or I challenge you to a duel to the death tomorrow morning."

"Above all else," the undisturbed American replied, "I want to know if your are prepared to quietly discuss this matter and to hear my explanations; if not it seems to me useless to continue our interview."

"Any explanation is useless in this situation and you have the choice of the two proposals I've made. Which do you choose?"

"Neither," answered Mr. Ward firmly.

"What!?" the stupified Fernando exclaimed.

"I ask you to give me your attention for just one minute, without in any way deterring yourself from behaving afterward in any way you please. I made a mistake, it is true, but while I'm no saint, I'm no satan either. I acted without proper forethought, and I regret it. Perhaps I behaved in the same way most men my age would have under similar circumstances. I am not guilty of betrayal, nor disloyalty, nor trickery. I never promised the young lady marriage; neither you nor anyone else can make the case that I deserted her. I never asked her to marry me and she never demanded that I marry her. I don't feel I betrayed the confidence of her family. I visited their home with the best of friendly intentions and sometimes I spent several days with them, always at their insistence."

"Because that honorable family extended its confidence to you, you are obliged to act the role of the gentleman."

"Well, you also visited the family," Mr. Ward noted coldly, "as a simple friend. Are you certain that you've never abused their confidence by permitting yourself some liberties with the young lady that could only be tolerated after the official announcement of a wedding?"

Fernando blushed, and the categorical denial he was about to give was stifled by his training to be civil in conduct and action. Still, despite the anger and indignation he felt, he did not dare protest because of the haunting memories of the scene at the theatre, the others at the farm, and his farewell to her the night before he left for exile.

While the Costa Rican stood frozen in silence, the Yankee continued, "Since she was free, I dared at the dance to express my sentiments that had been aroused that night by her beauty and my own decision to leave Costa Rica. She asked me to stay. Well, the rest was the work of fate, aided perhaps by the suggestions of a somewhat scatterbrained young lady. It is painful for me to recount some of the unpleasant details, but you put me in the difficult position of recalling them. Both young ladies acquired the habit of strolling every night alone close to my house. They would stop by the window of the billiard room where the boyfriend of Luisa and I played pool. We would go out to talk to them. . . . I invited them to come in. . . ."

"Don't excuse yourself by blaming the victim," Fernando exclaimed.

"Let's just for one moment reverse our roles," Mr. Ward continued. "Let's say I first approached that young woman and received from her proof of love; let's suppose also that you met her later and observed that she accepted your attentions. Tell me frankly: Would you ask her to marry you after you saw how easily she forgot in a few days and for no reason the man who first adored her?"

"In order to save her honor I certainly would."

"Not me," replied Mr. Ward phlegmatically. "A woman to save her reputation might accept the hand of a man who no longer either loved or respected her, but without love and respect their existence would be real hell for the two of them and prehaps even worse for her."

"What you mean," Fernando interjected with the same calm as his adversary, "is that you refuse to marry her because unfortunately in my country, unlike yours, they do not punish seducers and that you therefore select the second of my offers."

"No, not that one either. In this country people regard dueling as absurd. In fact, the law severely punishes it. Furthermore, the death of either one of us will solve nothing. Far from saving the young lady's reputation, it would only make public what until now is a secret carefully guarded by us.

Noticing that Fernando smiled disdainfully, he added, "I understand that you regard my refusal as a show of cowardice. While I fear the ridiculous, I fear no other man. Some six years ago in Mexico I accepted a bet and went alone along a road infested with bandits. Three assaulted me. I killed two; alas, I only injured the third. Check the newspapers of the time if you want to verify my story. If it's vengeance you want, attack me here or in the street, or better yet in some lonely spot. But I repeat, the death of one or both of us will not help matters one bit."

"If all your compatriots think as you do," the lawyer stated sarcastically, "they will not dare preach morality to the Latin Americans."

"If you're talking about dueling, I don't know; but if you're talking of seduction, who knows. I suppose it will depend on the temperament and circumstances of each person. At any rate, the one who dreamed up the flight from Costa Rica, the abduction of Miss Valdés, was not my fellow countryman."

The final retort struck Fernando like a knife in the chest. For a moment rage blinded him and he wanted to kill that cynical seducer on the spot. He realized though that any violence would only make matters worse for everyone. He checked his impulses. Approaching the desk, he said slowly, "When I can arrange things in such a way to punish you without hurting the reputation of the family that you've caused so much pain, I'll return expressely to kill you like a dog. You're a worthless man!"

He turned and left the office. Mr. Ward simply shrugged his shoulders and without even watching him leave reached out to pick up another letter from the pile and to continue the reading of his correspondence. The interview so upset Fernando that he wandered aimlessly through the streets of New York. Not until one in the morning did he return to the Hotel Astoria, to that same room he had occupied during his exile.

Despite the hatred he felt toward Mr. Ward, he appreciated that he was right about the futility of violence. It served no end. If the Yankee refused to marry Margarita, then what was the young lawyer to do? To kill him? Outside the satisfaction of vengeance what advantage would murder bring? Prison, perhaps the electric chair for him, and dishonor to the very family he hoped to defend. On the other hand, was Mr. Ward totally to blame as he had once imagined? Perhaps the young woman bore some or most of the blame herself because of imprudent conduct.

For a long time that question tortured Fernando like a poisoned arrow lodged in his heart, one he could not extract. How could he conceive such duplicity, such unheard of treachery in the woman who a few months earlier had given him so many proofs of her impassioned love? Upon realizing how unjustly and vilely he had been deceived, a bitter restentment seized him and he asked himself if it wasn't almost ridiculous to serve as the protector for a woman who had no consideration for him. Then, on the other hand, when he saw in his mind the pitiful image of the young women, the defenseless victim of inexperience and of the evil intentions of an unscrupulous adventurer, he felt inclined to pardon her as the thoughtless Helen of the Homeric epic had been pardoned.

A sense of justice ingrained in him from infancy told him that Mr. Ward, although cruel and ungentlemanly, had not been entirely devoid of insight and that Margarita did not deserve such harsh punishment, since her downfall was more the consequence of thoughtlessness than wickedness. He sat reflecting in an armchair in his room in that luxurious Astoria Hotel where a few weeks before he had received from Doña Virginia the first inkling of his misfortune. Fernando spent the rest of the night unable to sleep, just as he was unable to solve the heavy moral problems confronting him. At dawn he left for the wharf to take the steamship *Pastores* that weighed anchor at eight o'clock for a direct voyage to Costa Rica. Fernando leaned against the rail as the ship slowly departed. For a long time he soberly contemplated that despised land to which he swore he would never return.

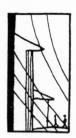

XIV

The Latin Heart

DIRECTING AND OVERSEEING the milking that four strapping young men had been working at between dawn and about nine o'clock, the trusted Fermín moved through the barn, first petting the quiet Holstein cows, then stroking or tickling the robust bulls, and finally scolding the men because they didn't properly clean the huge tin buckets in which they sent milk to the capital. For some weeks now he'd been quick tempered and grumpy, quite the opposite of his usual pleasant nature. This faithful servant could not explain the mysterious events occurring in the big house, a place he practically regarded as his own home. The sadness of his boss had affected him too. It was only natural that his boss's illness, that sudden paralysis which made him immobile and in need of others' help had affected the entire family, but why did the young mistress live secluded in her room and when she did appear on the porch or in the garden why was she so sad? Was it because her fiancée, that kind and noble youth, had stayed for only such a short visit when he returned from exile and then on the following day had left again? Was he the cause of all this trouble?

The simple thoughts of the overseer became lost in a labyrinth of conjectures, but because of his devotion to the Montalvos he did not mention any of his fears to the rest of the servants and workers.

That cold and rainy morning huge black clouds seemed to rise from the crater of Irazú Volcano. Slowly they covered the sky. A glacial wind buffeted them and chilled the air.

"Great god, what a freezing wind!" shouted one of the workers as he buttoned his jacket all the way to his chin. "This bucket of milk is as cold as ice."

Fermín, as soon as he had inspected the stalls and checked to see if the cows were fed, went out and stood under the cover of the eaves, a spot that offered a sweeping view of the road from San Isidro. Leaning against the barn he surveyed the vast scene. Suddenly he raised his hands to shield his eyes as if it might improve his vision. In the distance he could make out a small figure, almost a dot on the horizon, that was coming toward the estate. Slowly the figure became large enough so that Fermín would recognize the rider. He couldn't repress a shout of surprise and pleasure. It would be impossible to mistake that black and shining steed and the rider who handled it with elegance and spirit.

The overseer rushed down the path to the gate, arriving just as the rider reined his horse.

"Don Fernando! A sight for sore eyes! Are you all right? How was the trip?"

"Fine, Fermín," smiled the young man. "And how are you?"

"Getting along OK, thank God. He's certainly sent you here to see if you can cheer up this house."

"Listen, Fermín, I suppose Doña Virginia is awake already."

"Since five she's been cleaning the house and taking care of her pets. The boss has been in bed since the day before yesterday."

"Go in and tell her, but only her you understand, that I'm here and that I'd like to talk to her alone on the porch."

The overseer looked a little surprised but he rushed to carry out the order without even replying. Fernando dismounted, tied Menelik to a stall after taking off her bit and walked toward the house. At the top of the steps, Doña Virginia was already awaiting him. His face showed that unique and intimate pleasure of seeing a dear friend. But that kind old woman was much changed: the lines of her face had deepened, her hair was whiter; her body, once erect and agile despite the years, was bent over as though she shouldered a heavy weight; her eyes had lost their mischeiveous twinkle and the red eyelids told of long vigils and many tears. Fernando hugged her affectionately and without any polite conversation came right to the point.

"Doña Virginia, I need to see Margarita right away, even before I speak with Don Rafael. Just for a minute. That conversation will decide the fate of all of us."

So compelling was the tone of the lawyer that the old woman didn't dare even ask a question, let alone object. She asked him to wait there a moment while she went to her niece's room.

Considerable time passed. Alone on the porch, Fernando's eyes took in the familiar scene. Each object evoked pleasant memories, happy times that were now gone forever. The rattan furniture, the small lacquer tables, the baskets of plants, the beautiful garden below was a carpet of vivid colors, that giant tree that seemed to be such an intimate part of the family. . . . Everything now shrouded in a cloud of sadness. The tiny drops of water formed by the fog on the roses seemed to Fernando to be little tears shed in sorrow.

Finally Doña Virginia returned and informed him, "You may go in. She's waiting for you in her room. For the love of God, don't say anything to make her suffer any more than she is now."

Fernando followed Doña Virginia down the hall.

After knocking gently on the door, she opened it and then discretely withdrew.

At first Fernando saw nothing because with the shutters closed darkness bathed the room. Slowly he began to make out the shapes of the furniture and finally he caught sight of Margarita lying on the bed dressed in black with her head buried in the pillows to stifle her sobs.

Motionless in the center of the room, Fernando spoke in a quiet, tremulous voice, "Margarita, I'm not here to make any accusations nor to recall any memories from the past. I've come only to tell you that I did all I could to settle matters and to bring some piece of mind to you and your family. I failed. My trip was a waste of time. I had hoped to meet with a gentleman, and I encountered a rascal. However, I still hope I can relieve some of the sorrow. There is a way, although perhaps it might be too difficult for you. Agree to marry me."

His words astonished her. Mute with emotion, she turned her head for the first time to gaze on him with tear-drenched eyes.

"I guess I haven't made myself clear," he continued with grief. "Our marriage would be a pure formality. It would be a civil wedding; we would maintain separate quarters; soon thereafter I would leave for Europe and later you would have an excuse to seek a divorce. You'd then be free to select any man who could make you happy."

Margarita continued to stare at him as though she couldn't comprehend what he was saying. A deathly pallor covered her face, then she blushed, lowered her eyes and whispered between sobs, "Fernando, Fernando."

"Do you accept?" he repeated in a tone that was almost begging.

Then Margarita got up shaken by an indescribable emotion. Approaching him, she exclaimed with a heart-breaking voice, "No, I don't deserve generosity. I have no right to accept your sacrifice. Leave me alone in my disgrace. Why don't you kill me rather than forgive me. I'm vile, the vilest of women!"

"Calm down and think how we should face this situation. Will you give me permission to discuss my idea with your father?"

As her response, she grasped the hand of Fernando between both of hers. Then she leaned her head against the wall, put her handkerchief to her eyes and began to cry in silence.

Señor Montalvo was still in bed when Doña Virginia told him about the visit of the young lawyer. A ray of happiness lit his wrinkled face when he heard the news. Suspecting what the object of his friend's visit to New York had been, he assumed that Fernando brought back good news. He asked that he be admitted to his room at once. On seeing him, the old man exclaimed, "At this moment I feel the weight of my paralysis more than ever because it prevents me from giving you a warm, welcoming embrace."

"That doesn't matter. Just seeing you makes me feel that you've embraced me," answered Fernando giving him a warm, filial hug.

Then, without responding to the inquisitive looks of the old man, nor referring to the details of his trip abroad, he said in a grave and measured voice, "Don Rafael, I'm here for only one thing: to ask for Margarita's hand in marriage."

If at that moment Irazú had errupted, the old man wouldn't have been more stupified. He raised himself as best he could with his left arm and looking at the young man with his eyes wide open, he stammered, "You what! What are you saying! You . . ."

"I should have asked you ten months ago," said Fernando. "Perhaps it's my fault . . . but it's no use to talk of the past.

He spoke of his brief conversation with Margarita and explained the plan he'd devised. It was necessary to save the honor of the young woman, taking the quickest action possible to avoid any possible gossip. In order to make the sudden marriage comprehensible it would be necessary to follow a tightly constructed time table. Fernando would publish a fiery article in the newspaper attacking the program the new government had before congress. The very day Fernando had returned home from exile, the Minister of the Interior had warned him by means of an appropriate emissary that he was determined to exile Fernando again if he engaged in any politics, and since the lawyer knew that His Excellency never made vain threats, he was certain to be exiled the same day his article appeared. It wouldn't be difficult to get two or three days reprieve in order to marry, and thus there would be a perfect excuse to have a sudden marriage, one attended only by the family and without the prying curiosity of strangers.

When Fernando finished outlining his plan, Don Rafael, emotionally moved to the point of tears, strongly squeezed the young man's arm with his left hand and declared, "I've not been mistaken in my judgment of your character. Blessed be God who hasn't permitted the extinction of that old stock of Spanish nobility. Your nobility shines in this hour of infamy. How proud I would have been to have called you my son! But neither my daughter nor I can accept such a generous sacrifice because. . . ."

"Sacrifice! And what do I have to sacrifice?" a meloncholy Fernando questioned. "Hopes, a future, happiness, all are lost forever. I'm a useless link in the human chain and my last satisfaction will be to contribute to the happiness of a family I love very much."

It was extremely difficult to break the resistance of the old gentleman and perhaps Fernando wouldn't have succeeded without the able help of Doña Virginia, whose appropriate insights and persuasive eloquence weighed heavily in the decision-making of her brother. Finally he was convinced to confide the handling of that delicate matter to the intelligence of the young man, who departed for the city a few minutes later, with a promise to return on Sunday.

Dawn of the following day announced the end of the storm. The first rays of sunshine encountered not a single cloud in the sky and nature so dreary the day before awoke smiling like a young woman awakened by her husband's kiss. In the pastures, the colts displayed their happiness by running and prancing while their mothers called them with noisy neighing. The trees, quiet shadows the night before, were cathedrals of joyous sounds as the birds chirped in unison. In the barnyard the roosters crowed.

Fermín, who had feared the bad weather might endanger the health of the cattle, couldn't contain his joy, but his rejoicing knew no limits when he realized that another sun, no less splendrous, seemed to be shining within the house. That day, the young lady for the first time spent the entire morning in the garden; Don Rafael ate a hearty lunch under his fig tree, and Doña Virginia had recovered her jovial disposition.

Who could describe the enthisiasm of the loyal servant when that night he learned from the cook that Margarita would marry Fernando? Like all the gossiping villagers who observed the repeated visits of Mr. Ward a few months before, he had suspected that the American wanted to marry the daughter of the boss. Although he recognized the intelligence, skill, and energy of that foreigner, he didn't like the rude way he treated the workmen. Don Fernando was different. He commanded without offending his subordinates, without making them feel inferior. He was so good-hearted and so noble that everyone respected and liked him, Fermín in particular. He was very glad to learn that Fernando would soon be Don Rafael's son-in-law. Wasn't it Fernando who'd given him some money for medicines when one of his children was deathly ill? Wasn't it Fernando who'd given him his own hunting knife on the day they hunted turkeys?

To celebrate the happy occasion, the overseer brought

from his quarters a bottle of aguardiente and invited the other workers to share it. They gladly consumed it along with the coffee, chocolate, and cheese tortillas supplied by Doña Virginia.

Meanwhile in San José, Fernando didn't waste a minute in putting his plans into action. He began by converting his assets into liquid capital, which he deposited in the Bank of Spain because it was his intention to spend the rest of his life in either Madrid or Barcelona. He announced his forthcoming marriage,to the surprise of some of his relatives. Then, he published a broadside harshly attacking the government's program that had been submitted to Congress. The government reacted just as he had predicted. The very day his criticism was published, the government informed him he had twenty-four hours to leave Costa Rica. He wrote the Minister of the Interior at once to request an extension to seventy-two hours so that he could get married and arrange his business matters. He told the minister of his intention to abandon Costa Rica forever, news that made the official receptive to the request for the extension of time.

They held the civil marriage ceremony at El Higuerón. Don Rafael made a great point of telling his friends that Margarita wouldn't be able to accompany her husband into exile at that time. Because of delicate health, she wouldn't be able to resist the cold European winter.

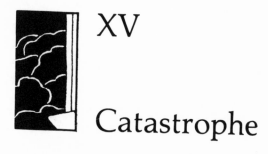

XV

Catastrophe

Only the most insensitive person would be incapable of understanding the deep sadness of a young man who felt alone in the world, buffeted by bad luck, suddenly put down in the midst of a large city. The impersonal nature of the large city isolated him more than if he were in the heart of a jungle or the center of a desert. If he'd been older he at least might have enjoyed the sterile satisfaction of having lived a good or bad life, and he could die comforted by the memory of happier periods in his life. But who can fathom the pain, the infinite pain, of one who in the prime of life sees his hopes and dreams collapse like a castle of cards that can never be rebuilt. Disappointments fatally wounded that youth. Desperate, he felt like a prisoner dragging a corpse at the other end of his chain. The human throngs that ebbed and flowed daily around Fernando in Barcelona hadn't the slightest suspicion that the young and arrogant body was the coffin of a soul broken into a thousand pieces. Dreams, love, fame, happiness! Everything was destroyed, pulverized instantaneously by a cruel fate.

To alleviate his boredom, the poor exile went by funicular almost every morning to the top of Tibidabo to view the blue Mediterranean below and to lose himself in contemplation of its beauty. The sea always attracts the dreamer and distressed because across its limitless and monotonous expanse both Fantasy and Pain can range freely. Each time that Fernando spotted among the tiny white sails of the fishing boats the dark silhouette of a transatlantic passenger ship, his thoughts raced across the ocean to the shores of his homeland, that country which had excluded him for the crime of loving it too much, that cruel, wretched, and unloving mother for whom he'd sacrificed his wellbeing, his future, and even his love. Never again would he set foot on those inhospitable shores!

He had struggled selflessly in order to save his people; he had valiantly denounced abuses and vices; he had fought against flattery, apathy, and the lack of civic valor; he had campaigned against those who turned the country into a scandalous marketplace, against the alienating education given youth; he had sounded the alarm to alert the nation that it was fatally falling into ruin and into the eager hands of foreigners. And for what? To see himself insulted by a corrupt press, abandoned by his friends, persecuted by the vengeance of those who enjoyed power and resentment of those below him, none of whom would pardon his brutal frankness. When he thought of his former colleagues who had once spoken out in favor of national morality and independence and who now kissed the very hand that had slapped their faces, revulsion seized him, and he swore never to return to his homeland until some worthy person cleansed its rottenness and cleaned its impurities.

One of the turncoats wrote him confidentially, inviting him to return home so long as he promised not to get involved in politics. He didn't even bother to answer the letter. He was determined never to go back. There was no reason to return to Costa Rica. What purpose could it serve? To struggle any further was useless; yet to resign himself to exist like a vegetable was impossible.

The woman to whom he'd pledged his heart forever had betrayed him, and by a supreme irony that woman now carried his name. Both society and law considered her to be his wife. He didn't love her now; he couldn't love her. Why then had he sacrificed his freedom for her? Why hadn't he broken with her once and for all? Why did he torture himself by looking for excuses to pardon her and to put all the blame on her seducer? Why did it bother him so much that very soon the child of that illicit passion would soon be born, an innocent being who would become an inseparable barrier between him and Margarita?

Of the few letters arriving from Costa Rica, he only enjoyed reading those from Doña Virginia and the ones Don Rafael wrote him through dictation to his daughter. Doña Virginia spoke, often in detail, of the sadness that enveloped El Higuerón and of the remorse and shame weighing on her niece whenever she thought of her past actions. Rafael, for his part, spoke sadly of his increasing infirmities and declining business, entrusted now to the honest but less efficient hands of Fermín.

When spring arrived with its carpet of flowers in the parks of Barcelona, Fernando received with an interval of two weeks two letters that together profoundly affected him. The first, from Doña Virginia, discretely informed him that the dreaded birth had occurred, but she added this sentence: "God in his mercy freed the poor little creature from serving as the constant reminder of her creation, and He decided that this innocent baby should not enter this world alive."

Dated two weeks later, the other letter was from Margarita. It read, "Fernando, I am daring to write you because I need to relieve some of my pain, and I should open my heart to you. Don't be afraid that I'm going to beg anything from you. I understand how much you must detest me, how little I must mean to you. You are right; I'm not worthy of you. You have been so noble and generous that your very goodness and pardon have been my worst punishment. How could I have been so wicked, so unworthy? I was insane, I swear it. I loved you with all my heart, only you; but my head was turned. I swear I don't know how. I never loved that man, never! I swear it. Was it his magnetism, suggestion. . . . I don't know. I can't account for what influenced me. Pardon these absurd ramblings. I only wanted to tell you that I have no right to continue ruining your future, your happiness. I can't permit you to continue your sacrifice for me. You are young and deserve to be happy. Throw off this burden, find an excuse, invent any reason to break this legal tie to me. I wouldn't know how to resolve it except by killing myself. God knows the only reason I haven't done it before is because I didn't want to give my father any greater grief. He would be so lonely and sick, the poor old man. If I am the only barrier standing between you and happiness why don't you free yourself from me? I will do whatever you want. I want to repay you at least a little of what I owe you and try to merit your pardon. Margarita."

After reading her letter, Fernando wandered aimlessly through the streets of Barcelona, much as he'd done in New York after his encounter with Mr. Ward. The profound emotion impelled him to move, as if the motion helped relieve his pain. That night he shut himself up in his bedroom to write a letter whose drafts he repeatedly tore up. It was a difficult letter to complete. Addressing the envelope, he looked at it strangely. Never in his life had he written that address. She bore his name; he'd never written her name as his. The next morning he carried that letter himself to the post office along with another to Don Rafael. Hailing a carriage afterward, he took a long drive through the city to Cortés Plaza where he got out in front of a lovely house surrounded by gardens. The newspapers had published an advertisement that it was for rent. He came to an agreement with the owner and signed the contract that afternoon.

During the following days, Fernando was busy preparing the house to suit his tastes. Carpenters, painters, carpet salesmen, all made their appearance. Although the house was furnished, the new renter still bought a lot of things for it. One of the purchases that stood out was a wheelchair and another was a large wooden statue, very well sculpted, of St. Rafael, to whom Doña Virginia was particularly devoted. With impressive elegance he arranged two of the rooms. In one of them he placed the saint within a luxuriously decorated niche, but in the other room he was even more elaborate in his preparations. It was so splendidly furnished and adorned that anyone could immediately tell that it would be inhabited by a young and elegant woman. Once his work was finished, he locked the house, put the key away and returned to his rather mundane habits. However, he showed a renewed liveliness as if those clouds that had so recently overshadowed his life had dissipated once and for all.

Alas, that serenity proved to be brief. Less than three weeks after he had sent the two letters, he received from Costa Rica one whose envelope trimmed in black announced mourning. Anxiety gripped Fernando as he tore it open. What new tragedy was this letter going to contain? His letter hadn't had time to be delivered yet; it was too early to expect an answer. Nervously he unfolded the letter and read:

"Fernando, Father is dead! He died the day before yesterday in a most horrible accident. We wanted to cable you, but service has been interrupted and probably won't be ready for another two weeks. I simply don't have the courage to suffer anymore. Every day my father spent a few hours seated under his fig tree where we would carry him in his chair. There he would read, and he didn't want us to disturb him until he called. Well, I was sewing in my room, while Mother worked in the kitchen. Suddenly I heard a great crash, the house trembled. Fearing it was an earthquake, I rushed out to see a sight that made me freeze in my tracks. I couldn't even scream I was so petrified. The fig tree had split in two, and when we rushed to the scene we found part of the trunk had fallen on Papa, injuring his head. He was alive but in great agony. He died a few minutes later without saying a single word. He didn't even recognize me. Why, why I asked, didn't that cruel tree fall on me. I'm the one who deserved that fate; I brought ruin and suffering to this house. Now I'm alone. Mother no longer talks to me, nor does anyone else. I'm alone. Margarita."

For some minutes Fernando remained desolate in his room with his hands over his eyes. What a strange turn of events. When he finally uncovered his face, his features showed no sign of his sorrow; instead, the crisis revealed in his face a firm decision to overcome all obstacles, to take action, and to resolve problems that had immobilized him. He understood the grief and pain of Margarita who had suffered so much already. She had become a victim, not unlike the heroine of the Greek epic, a victim of her own neuroses, of a corrupt society plagued with sexual permissiveness, of the aggressions of an insolent foreigner. As Fernando reflected on her fate, he sensed that it paralleled that of another victim, his own country. The two suffered similar fates. He had hoped that Costa Rica would be happy, propserous, and free; he found his homeland impoverished, violated, devoured by vice and exploitation, and pushed to the brink of ruin. He thought of his country as a beautiful garden abandoned by its owners and trampled by foreigners. He understood then that his place was in Costa Rica with his people. To live in exile, to remain alienated from them, was the equivalent of being a cowardly deserter.

For the first time, he realized the selfishness of his conduct. Through exile he had tried to evade his responsiblity as a citizen. He also had shirked his duties as a gentleman.

On the other side of the ocean, a young woman for whose disgrace he also bore some responsibility required his presence, just as his people needed his abilities to help redeem the nation. Fernando felt his faith renewed. He envisioned the future: It was a pleasant if distant scene of a rededicated life in the healthy environment of a happy home, a reconstructed household shaded and protected by a healthy and vigorous tree, the nation successfully regenerated by freedom, virture, and work.

With his thoughts clarified, Fernando nervously began to write, first a few lines to the owner of the house to arrange the cancellation of their contract and then a long telegram to Margarita. By telephone with the Spanish Steamship Office, he reserved a room aboard the *Monserrat*, due to depart early next week. He was returning to Costa Rica.

The Author: Carlos Gagini (1865-1925) was one of Costa Rica's leading writers. Writing during a period when the influence of the United States was increasing rapidly in Central America, he expressed the spirit of the new nationalism of the emerging urban middle class. With other Latin American writers from his generation he argued the spiritual superiority of Latin America over North American materialism, and he urged his countrymen to find their own solutions to their problems.

The Translator: E. Bradford Burns is Professor of History at the University of California at Los Angeles. A recognized authority on Latin America, he is author of many books on the region.

The Illustrator: Francisco Amighetti is a native of San José, Costa Rica. The line drawings reproduced in this book are taken from a portfolio of his drawings published in 1977 by the Editorial Universitaria Centroamericana (EDUCA). Most of them were displayed for the first time when the artist was living in Buenos Aires in 1932. His work has been displayed in the Museum of Modern Art in New York, the Palacio de Bellas Artes in Mexico City and in many other important museums and galleries.